Warwickshire County Council

03/14	HRB		
27-05/17	1 1 SEP 2021		
WHE			
5 JUL 2018			
2 4 JUN 2019			
2 9 NOV 2019			
1 0 NOV 2020			

This item is to be return[ed/r]enewed before the
latest date above. It ma[y be b]orrowed for a further
period if not in demand. To **renew your books:**

- **Phone the 24/7 Renewal Line 01926 499273 or**
- **Visit www.warwickshire.gov.uk/libraries**

Discover • Imagine • Learn • *with libraries*

Warwickshire County Council

Working for Warwickshire

THE
REBOUND GUY

THE REBOUND GUY

BY

FIONA HARPER

Published in Great Britain 2013
by Mills & Boon, an imprint of Harlequin (UK) Limited.
Large Print edition 2014
Harlequin (UK) Limited, Eton House,
18-24 Paradise Road, Richmond, Surrey, TW9 1SR

© 2013 Fiona Harper

ISBN: 978 0 263 24014 6

Printed and bound in Great Britain
by CPI Antony Rowe, Chippenham, Wiltshire

For everyone who has watched or is watching a loved one struggle with cancer. I wish you strength and peace.

CHAPTER ONE

KELLY'S FINGERS FROZE on her keyboard as a pair of warm hands rested on her shoulders. Around her the air stilled, but outside the office door the day went on as normal—the usual dull murmur of phones ringing, footsteps on the carpet, the high-pitched giggle of one of the secretaries.

'I'm almost finished typing this report,' she told the man standing behind her and shrugged her shoulders slightly. He didn't take the hint. Instead he leaned closer. She could feel the warmth of his cheek near hers and smell his expensive after-shave, yet he didn't turn and look at her. Instead he joined her in staring at the computer screen. It *could* have been innocent.

'I can see that,' he said softly, and his breath tickled her ear.

Kelly pressed the print button—no matter that she hadn't sorted out the formatting in the last couple of paragraphs—and pushed her chair back so she could slide out from underneath him and walk over to the printer on the other side of the room.

'Accounting called,' she said nonchalantly, deliberately not catching his eye. 'Shall I email a copy of this through to them?'

She could hear him walking, but she wasn't quite sure where he was. The last thing she wanted was to get ambushed again. That meant she needed to get a fix on him, and the only reliable way to do that was to look up.

Blast. She'd only been temping for Will Payne for a week and already she knew he took the most ridiculous things as encouragement. Eye contact being one of them. Not that he'd done anything truly inappropriate yet. There'd been the odd look, the occasional touch. Everything had been...borderline.

Some temps might have been overjoyed. He was in his mid-thirties, attractive, well-spoken and supposedly well-educated, but there was something about him... She glanced up, but avoided catching his gaze. He was walking towards her and when he came close enough, she handed him the pages the printer had spat out, using them as a shield.

'I knew you'd be an asset to my team as soon

as you walked through that office door,' he said smoothly. 'How about we go out for lunch to celebrate?'

Kelly blinked. 'Celebrate what?'

The report? That had taken all of forty-five minutes to sling together. Hardly worthy of a champagne toast.

'How about a long and successful working relationship?'

She swallowed. She was quite keen to improve her working relationship with the company—the HR manager had hinted they might be able to use her for at least another couple of months if she fitted in—but she'd rather keep her current boss at arm's length. Literally.

'I have a sandwich in my bag,' she said. 'Ham and mustard.'

Payne just smiled at her. He was enjoying this, damn him. Oh, she *so* wanted to tell him where he could shove his report—using graphs and pie charts and bulleted lists—but she needed this job. So instead she smiled and handed him the jumble of pages that had followed the others out of the printer.

'Come on,' Payne drawled, stepping close

enough for the sheets in Kelly's hand to curl back towards her chest. 'I know what you divorced girls are like…you get a taste of freedom and you go wild. Go on, live a little….'

Okay, so Will Payne had decided today was the day that *borderline* would be a distant speck in his rear-view mirror. Not good. Kelly clamped the pages to her chest, creating some space between them, and shook her head. 'Not my style,' she said politely. 'Really.'

He just grinned at her as if he didn't believe a word of it.

'It's true,' she said and ducked past him again, this time to place the now-crumpled second half of the report on his desk. 'I'm sorry, Mr Payne, but I think it's better for everyone if we keep our relationship strictly professional.'

Wow. Her brother would have been proud of her. She'd been as direct as always, but she'd actually managed to say what she wanted to say without using her tongue like a flame thrower. Wonders would never cease.

'Better for whom?' he said, leaning against the printer and looking her up and down in a manner that made her skin tingle. And not in a good way.

'Your wife, perhaps?' she said, looking him straight in the eye.

His expression faltered.

Watch it, Kelly. Just keep it inside for a few more minutes. Then you can take your lunch break, run up to HR and stage a sit-in until they agree to move you somewhere else in the company. There was no way she was going to be able to outrun Will Payne for the next few months, and she shouldn't have to even try.

She'd been telling the truth. She hadn't had any time for men since her divorce—she'd had much more serious stuff to deal with. And, to be honest, this man reminded her a little too much of her ex. He'd had that same swagger, that same self-assurance. The same urge to flirt wired into his DNA.

'I think I'll take my lunch now, if you don't mind,' she said, backing away.

He strolled towards her, a predatory look in his eye. 'Come on, Kelly…' he said, lowering his eyelids slightly. 'You look like a girl who knows how to have a little fun.'

Kelly was close to his large, rather nice oak desk. She circled it, feeling a lot better once the solid hunk of wood was between them, but he followed her round and placed his hand on her arm, before letting it slide down the sleeve of her blouse. She slipped away before his knuckles could graze the side of her left breast, quickly completing her circuit of the desk. She hoped desperately he'd drop into his high-backed leather chair when he reached it, but he didn't take his eyes off her. He also didn't stop walking.

Seriously? He was *actually* on the verge of chasing her round the desk?

She didn't want to lose this job, but there were lengths she was not prepared to go to to keep working at Aspire Sports, even if it was a temp's dream—a vibrant young company that was going places, with good wages and enough departments to mean she really might manage to skip from one to another, filling gaps as needed. Another few months of this kind of salary and she'd be able to save enough to finally start looking for a house, then she and the boys would have a real home again.

But thinking of a new house just reminded her of the old one she'd been forced to move out of, and just how callous Tim had been about it, how he'd been too busy enjoying his so-called freedom to think about the upheaval he'd caused their two children. Kelly started to march rather than walk, to glare rather than stare back neutrally. This man was cut from the same cloth, and she found herself channelling all the unresolved anger from the last few years in his direction.

He was back on his side of the desk now, beside his chair, and she was on the side nearest the door. She stopped walking, braced her hands on the desk and leaned forward just a little.

'Listen, *Mister* Payne. I'm not interested. I've said so repeatedly, and your behaviour is totally inappropriate. If you don't stop trying to get your grubby little hands on me, I'm going to lodge a formal complaint.'

One side of his mouth hitched up, then he started to speak.

She decided not to wait to hear what he had to say—or give him a chance to start moving again. She leaned forward, forgetting that it would give him an even better view of her cleavage. 'You just stay on your side of the desk, or else!'

His gaze drifted downward before returning to her face. There was the most annoying little twinkle in his eye. She was seriously tempted to see if a right hook could dislodge it, but that would just get her arrested. And, more importantly, fired.

Her soon-to-be ex-boss cocked an eyebrow. She assumed he was trying to look appealingly naughty. This guy was not taking her seriously and that was really starting to tick her off.

'Or else what?' he asked and matched her position, placing his palms on the wooden desk top and leaning in close so their mouths were only inches apart.

Kelly just smiled a slow, sweet smile, and then she leaned forward and showed him.

Jason Knight balanced a minibasketball on the fingers of one hand and fixed his focus on the equally small hoop on his office wall. There was a moment of complete stillness then, with a flick of his wrist, he sent ball flying towards hoop. It sailed through the air then dropped neatly through the ring. He smiled at the satisfying rustle of knotted string as the ball passed through it and landed on the floor. He went to retrieve it, then repeated the process a few more times.

If anyone had been watching, they'd have thought he was goofing around, killing time in the middle of a busy business day, but that was far from the case. Some people got their best ideas doing mundane, repetitive activities, like ironing or walking the dog. Shooting hoops helped him think.

Back home they'd had a hoop secured above the garage door in the front yard. It was the one thing he really missed about home, but this side of the Atlantic it was all about soccer, something he'd never really gotten into. He sighed and lined the ball up again. He'd already shot twenty times and had only missed three, yet he still was no closer to solving his problem.

Dale McGrath was proving to be a very hard man to get hold of, and he really, really wanted to set up a meeting with the guy. Jason knew he could find another athlete to endorse his new range of high-performance running shoes if he really wanted to, but Dale's face had appeared in his mind during his *other* good thinking activity— swimming laps—and he knew the straight-talking Olympic gold medallist was the right figurehead for the product. If McGrath took his shoes seriously, then everyone else would too.

And not only would it be a coup for the company, but it would prove once and for all to his father that he wasn't just 'messing around' in the family toys and games business.

Eight years ago the old man had sent him here to head up the struggling London-based sports equipment company he'd just bought out. Jason suspected his father had just given up trying to get his wayward son to do things his way and had shipped him off to keep him out of his hair. But, hey, who needed Jason when his younger, golden-haired brother was around to worship? He released the ball again, but this time he put a little too much force behind it and it bounced off the wall, wide of the hoop.

He grunted and placed his feet firmly on the floor so he could go and retrieve it but, before he could stand up, his office door banged open. He looked up to find his HR manager marching towards him. She slapped a crisp-looking white envelope down on the desk in front of him.

He frowned. 'What's that?'

Julie was looking seriously flustered. One hair on her neatly groomed salt-and-pepper head was standing to attention. It was the untidiest he'd ever seen her look.

'My resignation letter,' she said, crossing her arms.

Jason stared at it. Julie threatened to resign at least three times a month, but she'd never got as far as producing stationery before. 'Okay...' he said slowly.

'No, it's not okay! Down in my office, I've got yet another temp in tears. You can't believe the amount I've spent on boxes of tissues in the last two months!'

'Ah.' Jason peered round Julie to the anteroom where his PA normally sat. He'd wondered why it had been so quiet out there. He guessed the 'little chat' he'd had with Felicity last night hadn't gone down well.

'Yes, *ah*. It's been a nightmare since Katrin resigned! You've been through six temps in just over two months. Six! And I can't spend all my time trawling the employment agencies of London just to keep you in dates on a Friday evening. I've been with this company twenty years and never before have I felt my job description involved being the boss's pimp!'

Okay, so this wasn't just another idle threat. Julie was really upset. Which was a pity, because he'd been having quite a good time since his girlfriend and permanent PA had decided to leave both him and the company. He'd been working long hours and there'd been a steady parade of pretty young women flowing through his office. Who *wouldn't* have taken advantage of such a gift?

It wasn't as if he'd done all the running, either. One or two had practically launched themselves across the desk at him. It was just that they hadn't wanted to hear he wasn't interested in turning the job—or the relationship—into a long-term fixture that had got them all weepy. But he'd never broken a promise or led them to believe otherwise. It was hardly *his* fault if women decided to get all kinds of strange notions in their heads.

Julie was tapping her foot. 'Well?' she said, raising one eyebrow, the only part of her that wasn't starched and stiff. Julie had surprisingly mobile eyebrows. All the more noticeable for their slight bushiness…

Jason smiled at her, turning it on full beam. He knew Julie was the one woman in the universe who seemed to be immune to it, but it couldn't hurt to try and buy himself a couple more seconds of thinking time. 'Will "I'm sorry" do?' he asked hopefully.

Julie just snorted.

That caused Jason to get a little more serious. She'd been with Aspire for more than two decades, and when he'd arrived off the plane from New York as a clueless twenty-something, annoyed his only option had been to cave in and do what his father had told him for once, Julie had taken one look at him and told him to stop acting the poor little rich kid and get over himself. His father had sent him half a world away and he didn't like it much—so what? There was a whole company nervous about the takeover, and they'd needed him to step up to the plate and turn it around. Their jobs, their families, depended on him, she'd said. It was Julie who'd given him a much-needed kick up the pants and made him realise that proving his father wrong about being a waste of space might be much more satisfying than proving him right.

So, while his HR manager might have battery acid for saliva, Jason couldn't afford to lose her. She'd been both his harshest critic and his biggest cheerleader, and what she didn't know about the UK sports equipment industry wasn't worth knowing. Without Julie, Aspire wouldn't be the up-and-coming company it was today, which meant he owed her. Big time.

For a second, just a second, he let down the permanent sheen of 'nothing sticks' he always wore and softened his gaze. He looked Julie in the eye. 'You can't leave,' he told her. 'I don't know what I'd do without you.'

She rolled her eyes, but dropped into the chair on the other side of his desk and looked away.

He nudged the envelope towards her. 'Please?' he said. 'Take this back and shred it.'

She reached for it and pulled it towards her, but drew her hand away again when the envelope was half off the edge of the desk. 'Not so fast.' She folded her arms across her considerable cleavage. 'There are some conditions to the destruction of this letter.'

Jason slumped back in his chair and sighed. He had a feeling he wasn't going to like these 'conditions' much. 'Fire away,' he said wearily.

The hint of a victorious smirk played on Julie's lips. 'One…no more flirting with the temps—that's how the whole mess begins.'

Jason tried not to smile. Okay, so he'd calm down

a little. That didn't mean he couldn't be receptive if an attractive woman flirted with him, now, did it? However, Julie spotted the microscopic twitch of his lips and her eyes narrowed.

'Two...' she said slowly '...no encouraging anyone employed by Aspire to flirt with you.'

You're a statue, he told himself. Don't react.

'Or letting them flirt with you unprovoked.'

Dammit.

'And definitely no physical contact with your employees.'

He raised his eyebrows and tried to look wounded. 'What? Not even a friendly clap on the shoulder between buddies, a handshake at the beginning or end of a meeting...?'

Julie's scowl intensified. 'Don't push it, Jason! You know exactly what I mean. I'm talking about female employees—unless you've worked your way through the whole office and are thinking of going a different direction?'

He grinned and shook his head. Nope. Definitely not tired of women yet. 'So are handshakes allowed?' he asked innocently.

Julie peered at him a little more closely, as if she

was trying to work out what was going on in his head. 'Handshakes are allowed,' she finally said.

Jason nodded. A concession. No, a victory. It was always important to win something in negotiations; he just didn't know how he was going to use this to his advantage. Yet.

Julie uncrossed her arms and let out a breath. 'Good.' She shook her head. 'I don't know why you can't just find one woman you like enough to stick with for more than a weekend.'

Jason stood, then went and retrieved the mini-basketball from where it was still resting against the window. 'It's not liking them enough that's the problem,' he said as he rolled it into his palm and turned to face her. 'It's liking them too much. There are so many amazing women out there—'

She made a face. 'Spare me.'

'There's nothing wrong with having a little fun while I'm still young.' Then, just to make her feel better, he added, 'But maybe I will settle down... one day.'

'My Jonathan is three years younger than you and he's already got a toddler and another one on the way. Now, if that's all,' she said, swiping her letter off his desk and heading for the door, 'I've got one soggy temp to deal with and another who's asked for an appointment. She sounded spitting mad…'

She stopped at the doorway and peered over the top of her glasses at him. 'That hasn't got anything to do with you, has it? Two in one day is a record, even for you.'

Jason just chuckled as she turned and marched out of the office. *Oh, Julie. If only you knew…*

'She did what?' the HR manager stuttered as her underling repeated the story Kelly had just told her. She swung round to face Kelly. Julie was wearing the look of a woman who was not having a good day. 'You did *what*?'

Kelly folded her hands in her lap and looked the woman straight in the eye. 'I stapled his tie to the desk.'

Julie's mouth moved but no sound came out.

'It was the only way I could make him stay where he was supposed to,' Kelly added helpfully. 'I'm sorry about the desk, but Mr Payne wouldn't take no for an answer. So I made him.'

That would teach him to not take her seriously.

The underling had to turn away and stifle her

giggles behind a hand. Julie blinked a few times then seemed to recover herself. 'Well, of course we'll investigate your complaint, Ms Bradford, but there are ways to go about this kind of thing. Ways that don't involve office equipment....' She lowered her chin and looked at Kelly over the top of her glasses.

Kelly nodded, the picture of innocence. No point telling the woman she'd have liked to staple something else of Payne's to the desk and the tie had just been a poor substitute. 'Thank you.'

The underling sighed. 'You know, a lot of girls think Will is a bit of a hottie.'

Well, a lot of girls needed their heads read.

Kelly didn't say that, though. She was busy proving she could be calm and professional and that she could keep control of her runaway mouth—and her stapling arm. She settled on something much less inflammatory. 'But I'm just not interested. In him, or anyone.' She frowned. 'Isn't there a company policy against that kind of thing?'

'Mr Knight did away with that,' Julie said starchily, as she and the underling exchanged a cryptic look. 'He says he doesn't want the company stuck in the Dark Ages, and that as long as his staff do their work well he doesn't care what they get up to in their personal lives.'

On any other day Kelly would have applauded the boss's decision heartily. Today, however, a medieval dating policy—maybe involving male chastity belts?—might have made her life a little bit easier. 'Well, *I* have a personal policy about dating colleagues,' she said.

Julie gave Kelly a sceptical look then sat back down at her desk and leafed through her file. When she'd finished, she looked at her over her glasses again. 'You've been with us just under a month and this is the third time we've moved you….'

'I can explain about—'

Julie just raised her eyebrows. 'It seems you don't have a problem speaking your mind, Ms Bradford, which I wouldn't normally consider a bad thing, but you do manage to rub people the wrong way. I'm wondering if we even have anywhere we can usefully place you immediately.' She squinted at the computer screen and reached for her mouse. 'We *might* have another position for you….' However, the tone of her voice suggested she was just going through the motions.

Kelly's smile remained fixed, but inside her

stomach dropped. She couldn't let them send her
back off to the temp agency and give someone else
the position.

The other woman shook her head. 'No…sorry.
Nothing suitable, really.' She looked up and gave
Kelly a tight smile. 'Of course, we'll contact your
agency if anything opens up.'

Kelly stood up. 'Look, this just isn't fair! I'd have
happily worked hard for Will Payne if he'd acted
appropriately. I shouldn't be the one who's penal-
ised!'

Julie looked at Kelly's recently vacated chair,
and it took all Kelly had to plant her bum back
down on it.

'It's not about punishment, Kelly,' Julie said, a
hint more sympathy in her tone. 'You know how
temp work goes…We do need some short-term
cover for a couple of the senior management team,
but those posts require a certain level of skills—'

'I have skills,' she said firmly.

'And a certain level of…sensitivity,' Julie added.
Ah.

'Please,' Kelly said quietly, hating the slightly
scratchy tone that had crept into her voice. 'I
really need another chance. I'll do anything, work

for anyone… You won't hear a peep of complaint from me, I promise.' Her voice caught on the last few words.

Oh, hell. Here came the waterworks. Great.

Kelly wasn't normally one for crying. In fact, it had been months since she'd had a good bawl, but every time she thought she was recovering from the events of the last couple of years, life dumped another obstacle in her path. To be honest, she was exhausted, and maybe the game of kiss chase she'd had with Payne this morning had just been the cherry on the cake. She scrabbled around in her handbag for a tissue. There had to be one somewhere! Essential piece of kit when you were mum to two boys under six.

Drat. She couldn't find one. And then she remembered why; she'd used them all up wiping mud off Ben's fingers before she'd dropped him off at her brother's house. Seems Ben had decided his uncle's front garden was a good place to dig for worms, and she hadn't wanted him to get muddy fingerprints on her new sister-in-law's cream sofa.

She sniffed back as much as she could and swiped at her face with her hands. Julie leaned across the desk and offered a tissue from a pink box covered in cartoon cats. Kelly took the last one, and Julie tutted and sighed before throwing the empty box in the waste paper basket. The underling rummaged in a drawer, produced an identical box and placed it on the corner of the desk. It had the feeling of a well-oiled routine.

Julie's tone was much more sympathetic when she spoke. 'It'll be okay. You'll find something else. Aside from the…ah…personnel problems, your work has been top-notch.'

Kelly shook her head. 'It's not just that…'

Another sniff. One that gurgled. *Nice.* She blew her nose.

She could handle the job thing. She was strong. A survivor. Everyone said so. And she didn't want this woman to think she was a snivelling ninny.

'Sorry,' she said, composing herself and sitting up straighter. She needed to get back control of this situation, and the best way she knew how was with the bald truth. 'It's just been a rough couple of years. My husband ran off with his twenty-two-year-old personal trainer just after I was diagnosed with cancer, so you can see why I'm not particularly keen on the male species at the moment.' She looked up and met Julie's gaze. 'I'm okay now, though—scans clear for over a year—but I couldn't work for a while and I had to sell the house....' She waited for a moment while the stinging sensation in her nose faded. 'This job at Aspire was going to help me save up for a new one, so I would just really, really appreciate it if you'd give me a call if something new opens up.'

She hid the crumpled tissue in her clenched hands, placed them in her lap and waited. The manager and her underling stared back at her, jaws a little slack. Her no-varnish story had taken them by surprise. Good. Kelly started to feel as if she was on level ground again.

No one said anything for a few long seconds. Then Julie cleared her throat and leaned forward. 'Were you serious when you said you would ab-solutely, categorically *not* date someone at work?'

Kelly nodded, even though the question con-fused her. Hadn't they said that was fine?

'And do you think you can bring some of that gumption you've just shown me into the office each day, starting Monday? Because you're really going to need it if I give you this chance.'

Kelly nodded even harder. Bringing it with her

wasn't a problem; it was keeping it locked away that was the struggle.

'Then, Ms Bradford,' Julie said, giving her what *might* have been a smile, 'I think I have the perfect post for you.'

CHAPTER TWO

MONDAY MORNING AND Jason was thinking again.
Thinking hard. He balanced the minibasketball on
his fingertips and narrowed his eyes as he visu-
alised the ball dropping through the net, then he
tensed his arm muscles in readiness and...

There was a sharp rap on the office door. The
ball soared across the room and crashed into the
bookcase, sending a photo of him with his father
and younger brother plummeting to the floor.
'What?' he barked out.

The door nudged open and a woman he didn't
recognise poked her head through. 'Mr Knight?'

Jason forgot all about the photograph. He forgot
all about the half-size basketball rolling along his
office floor. He spun his chair round to face the
door, sat up straighter and smiled. Women loved
his smile. 'You found him.'

She scanned the room, found both fallen photo
frame and ball then looked at him without smil-

ing back. 'Human Resources sent me up. I'm your new temporary PA.'

Jason's grin widened. 'Come on in, then.'

He bounced to his feet and waited for her to cross the room. Normally, he was an impatient sort of guy. He didn't like to stand around doing nothing, but at this present moment he really didn't mind that he was rooted to the spot. The woman who walked across the carpet towards him was his favourite office fantasy: tall, long legs, glossy hair caught back in a low, short ponytail. She was wearing the standard temp uniform of white blouse, dark skirt, stockings and heels. Wowzer.

He loved the sexy librarian type—all reserve and manners until you said or did the right thing and then they transformed into a wildcat right before your eyes…or under your touch. Jason swallowed the pool of saliva that had collected under his tongue.

But then he heard Julie's voice, crisp and clear, inside his head. *No flirting.* Damn.

'Jason Knight,' he said, extending his hand over the desk. 'How are you finding Aspire?'

See? Nothing flirty about that.

'Kelly Bradford. And it's been an eventful couple of weeks.' She made it sound as if that wasn't a good thing.

She stared at his hand for a moment. He could tell she didn't want to shake it, but thankfully the British gene for politeness hijacked her and she lifted her arm. They both leaned forward to reach over the wide desk, and Jason realised the top button of her blouse was directly in his line of sight. It wasn't straining; both blouse and button were perfectly respectable. The fastening wasn't even low enough to give a tantalising glimpse of cleavage, but he felt his blood pressure hitch all the same. He'd always liked buttons and the sense of promise that came with them, but when had they become so totally absorbing?

He should look away, shouldn't he? He should make this a momentary, almost unconscious, glance and meet her gaze. And he would. Soon.

'If you've finished staring down my blouse, I wondered if you'd tell me what you'd like me to do first,' she said with a hint of frost in her tone. Was it wrong that he liked that even more?

Probably.

The tractor beam that had been holding his head in position suddenly released him, and he found himself staring back at her. Her chin tilted higher and there was fire in those eyes. Lesser guys would have blushed and stuttered. Jason just stared right back.

Okay…so he'd been wrong about the librarian thing. This one was a wildcat. And still as sexy as hell. Now he was intrigued to find out if there was a softer, more feminine side to her under the bristling exterior.

He marshalled his features into the picture of seriousness. She'd been blunt and honest and he figured she'd respect it if he responded in kind. And he couldn't get into trouble with Julie for that. Flirting was full of little lies—a smile that was too bright, a touch of an arm that was manufactured rather than an instinctive response, the leaving out of tiny unflattering details—so this definitely wasn't flirting.

'I apologise for my wayward eyeballs,' he said. 'What can I say? I'm a guy, and sometimes they act on their own, without a command from the main control centre.' He tapped a finger to his skull to make his point.

Her eyes narrowed slightly. 'Oh, *that's* the main control centre, is it?' she said, her voice thick with sweetness. 'I always thought men used that space for storing useless sports statistics and all the decisions were made much further south.'

Ouch. True, but *ouch*.

He grinned. 'I do my best to rise above my biology.'

Her features didn't move. 'You need more practice. Now…I'd like to do something more productive than stand here and chat about what's south of your belt buckle… I don't suppose you have any actual work you want me to do, do you?'

Jason threw his head back and laughed, which seemed to take his new PA completely by surprise. The hard edge disappeared from her expression and she just stared at him.

'Julie was right. I can see you and I are going to get on just fine.'

He saw a hint of surprise behind those intelligent grey-green eyes. And relief. He realised she'd maybe come out with all guns blazing because she was nervous. He was the boss, after all. But Kelly Bradford had showed guts and quick wit, both qualities he liked in a woman.

Darn this new no-flirting policy of Julie's!

But he was going to have to live with the agreement he'd made. Thanks to the merry-go-round of different PAs he'd had for the last couple of months, progress on the McGrath deal had stalled and he needed to get it back on track. Maybe hanging on to one for more than a fortnight would help.

He picked up a folder that had been sitting on his desk and handed it to Kelly. 'I'd like you to familiarise yourself with the Mercury shoes project. I'm in the process of setting up a meeting with a few sports personalities who I hope will endorse the shoes when we launch. We need a kick-ass presentation to convince them to take a chance on a new brand in the market.' If that didn't open the hallowed doors of McGrath's office to him, he didn't know what would.

She took the folder from him and hugged it to her chest, once and for all preventing any possibility of him being distracted by that top button.

'Right,' she said and backed away a few steps. 'Will do.' And then she turned and walked from the room, closing the door behind her.

Those curves in that skirt? Pure magic. Jason had enjoyed the view while it lasted, but he hoped his HR manager didn't have as much divine authority as she claimed to have, or he was in danger of being fried by a lightning bolt from the sky.

Kelly walked back to her desk on shaky feet. Once there she collapsed into her chair and stared blankly at the computer screen, still clutching the folder Jason had given her to her chest. What the hell had just happened back there?

Her boss had flirted with her, that was what.

That wasn't new, especially after that episode with Payne last Friday, but she hadn't expected it to become the norm.

She didn't get it. She'd always had a certain amount of attention from the male species, but in the last couple of months it had gone to a whole new level, which was weird, because for a while after her chemo had finished she'd wondered if she'd ever feel attractive again.

Maybe it was because the words 'not interested' were practically dancing over her head in neon lights. Men always seemed to want what they couldn't have, and she was projecting that out into the universe with a fury.

Her new boss had flirted with her. So what?

Kelly hugged the folder even tighter to her chest, causing a couple of pages at the open side to curl.

She'd wanted to flirt right back. That was what.

She hadn't, though. Which felt like a victory, although she didn't know why. She let out a slow breath and placed the slightly creased folder on the desk in front of her.

As she'd stepped into the room and walked towards him the energy he projected had been tangible. The air had practically hummed with it. She wanted to catch some of that stuff and bottle it, save it for the times when she was on her own at the end of the day, a struggling single mother with two small boys who'd developed a complex and effective strategy to avoid bedtime, the times when she was just so weary she couldn't quite remember her own name.

Maybe that was it. Maybe it hadn't been a physical thing at all. It had just been that drive and dynamism that had attracted her. She'd used to have buckets of that—once. Where had it all gone?

But then she thought about Jason's dark, slightly unruly hair, those laughing blue eyes and those lips…those lips that just begged to be…

Kelly felt a jolt of warmth deep inside that had nothing to do with energy levels.

Blast. Just when she'd been halfway to talking herself out of it too.

She'd done her best to rein in what she'd been feeling when she'd been in there, despite the fact that although she'd stood as straight as a poker on the outside, something inside had gone soft and gooey, and she'd almost felt as if she'd been leaning towards him, curving invitingly...

Kelly lowered her head and rested it so her brow made contact with the folder she'd just placed on her desk. Oh, hell. Maybe she'd just been too long without a man. It had been almost three years since she'd split from Tim and there hadn't been anyone else.

Yet, a small but optimistic voice in the back of her head reminded her. There hasn't been anyone else *yet*.

Whatever.

It had been a long time. And how was a girl supposed to keep her head about her when she walked into a room and came face to face with Jason Knight? All that testosterone, those broad shoulders—hadn't she heard he'd been a swimmer

once?—that lazy smile lit up with wickedness…
It had all been too much for her poor sex-starved
circuits and they'd gone into overload.

She inhaled and sat upright again. Right. She had
a job to do. She couldn't sit here impersonating a
jellyfish all day. Especially as she'd got the sense
from Julie in HR that this was her last chance.
She had to make this post work for the next few
months. Her nest egg depended on it.

She blew out a breath and turned on her computer. There was plenty of work to do. And more
interesting jobs than the stuff Payne had given her,
that was for sure. She'd just bury herself in that
and forget about the man on the other side of the
office door.

A thud from inside made her jump. She went
very still.

A very thin office door, it now seemed.

What had just happened? Had he knocked something over, fallen off his chair? She was just de-
bating whether she should go and check on him
when the noise came again. And then, a few moments later, again.

The basketball.

Thud.

Kelly flinched in her seat.

Great. If he was going to keep this up all day, she'd never have a chance of forgetting his existence and getting on with her work. Her forehead met the desk again. Lord, oh, Lord, what had she and her big I'll-take-any-job-you-offer-me mouth got her into now?

Kelly waited outside her brother's front door after pressing her thumb to the doorbell. The silence lasted a split second and then there was the thunder of little feet and squeals of *'Mummy!'* in the hallway. On the commute, tiredness had set around her like concrete, but now it cracked and started to crumble.

Moments later her sister-in-law opened the door and Kelly bent down to greet her two boys. It was more like being hit by a pair of charging bulldogs than being hugged, but she smiled and kissed the tops of their heads before they ran off back to a room where a television was blaring. She stood up and smiled wearily at Chloe.

'Thanks for looking after them today. That's the one downside of temping—patchy work can mean patchy childcare.'

Chloe smiled back and shrugged. 'No problem.'

'I spoke to my usual childminder earlier and she says she can pick up again from tomorrow.'

Chloe stood back so Kelly could pass by, closed the door then followed her into the large kitchen-diner at the back of the house. 'Well, let us know if you need us again. I think Dan misses the boys since you moved out.'

Kelly had lived here for more than a year after she'd sold the house. Her brother had been great, but when she'd felt well enough she'd insisted on branching out on her own. All the time she'd been relying on him she'd felt as if she hadn't quite finished her recovery, and that hadn't been good. She really, really needed to feel as if she was moving on, putting the nightmare of the last few years behind her.

Chloe headed for the fridge. 'I know it's only Monday, but you look like you've had one hell of a week.' She pulled a bottle of pinot grigio out of the fridge door and poured them both a glass. 'I didn't think it could get much worse than what you told me happened last Friday, but you look a bit… frazzled…this evening.'

Kelly chuckled and slumped onto a stool at the

breakfast bar. Her sister-in-law was too polite. She knocked back a good long slug of wine. 'What you mean is that I look like I've been run over by a truck.'

'You look fine,' Chloe said soothingly. 'Just tired. Please don't tell me the new boss has been doing circuits round the desk with you too!'

Kelly shook her head. More to dislodge the mental image that had suddenly warmed her ears than to disagree.

'Well, that's a relief!' Chloe said, laughing.

Kelly didn't join her.

'What's he like—the big boss?'

Kelly swallowed. Tall. Broad. With thick dark hair and a twinkle in his eye that could light kindling....

'Oh, he's okay,' she said, looking down into her glass and swilling the wine around.

When she looked up again Chloe was smiling at her. 'More than okay, I reckon.'

'I didn't say anything of the sort,' Kelly said stiffly.

Her sister-in-law sighed. 'You didn't have to, Kells. It's written all over your face. You're a terrible liar, you know.' She grinned. 'He's nice, isn't he?'

'No.'

And this time Kelly was telling the truth. *Nice* was definitely not a word she'd use to describe Jason Knight.

Chloe smiled even wider. 'But you like him anyway....'

Kelly resorted to silence. And more wine.

Like was also the wrong word to use to describe what she felt for her new boss. It had been pure and unadulterated lust, that was all.

That was *all*?

The silence didn't last long. It never did. Not when Kelly had uncomfortable thoughts running round her head that she needed to expel. 'Okay, maybe I *liked* him.' She wasn't prepared to use another word just yet. That one, for all its wishy-washiness, was scary enough. 'Maybe I haven't felt that way for a long while.'

She paused to take another sip of wine. Chloe put her elbows on the counter, rested her chin in her upturned hands and sat there looking receptive. Kelly didn't make her wait long. 'And maybe I hadn't felt that way since well before I split with

Tim, but that doesn't mean anything... Don't give me that look, Chloe! It wasn't a sign from on high. Just my hormones getting in a fizz over a nice-looking guy.'

But it would have been a whole lot easier to believe her own pep talk if she wasn't actually both relieved and pleased about the strong physical reaction she'd had to her new boss.

'It just took me by surprise,' she added. 'I haven't told you this, but for a long while I've been a bit worried about my lack of interest in the opposite sex. I wondered...I thought...' She looked Chloe in the eye. 'I was afraid the chemo had fried that bit of me. I felt like someone had turned something off inside me, that I was broken somehow.'

'But you're not,' Chloe said sympathetically and firmly.

'Yup. And now everything's okay. I'm all fixed again. That's all I need to know.'

Chloe topped up Kelly's glass. 'So why don't you do something about it?'

Kelly's residual head-nodding turned to shaking. 'Not a good idea.'

'Because...?'

Kelly stood up and walked over to the other side

of the kitchen, glass in hand. 'Did you not hear last week's story, with the sleazy boss and the desk…?'

'You wouldn't have that glow in your cheeks if you thought he was sleazy and, from what I can gather, he's got a steady job, money in the bank and he's rather easy on the eye. Much better than most of the single men out there in their thirties.'

Kelly wanted to disagree with that, but her sister-in-law had a point.

'And the problem with Mr Sleaze was that you didn't like him back. You've already said you're attracted to your new boss. Does *he* like *you*?'

Kelly sighed and clutched her wine glass to her chest. 'He couldn't stop staring at my breasts when we first met, so I'd say that's an affirmative.'

Chloe sat up and clapped her hands lightly together. 'That's decided then.'

'Nuh-uh,' she said, and walked down the hallway to check on the boys, who were still watching TV. When she came back she sat back down on a stool, faced Chloe and put her glass down. 'Not only is he the boss, but he's got a bit of a reputation as a player. He's no good for the long-term.'

'Who mentioned anything about long-term?' Chloe sipped her wine and looked at Kelly from under her lashes. 'Keep it short and sweet—you set the rules, you set the timing… Sounds like the perfect rebound guy to me. You're long overdue one of those.'

Kelly snorted. 'You're out of your mind! It's still a recipe for trouble and I *need* this job.'

'No, you don't,' Chloe said. 'You've got enough savings for a deposit. Why wait? You should be out there looking for a nice little house. Don't tell me you're as scared of house-hunting as you are of man hunting.'

'I'm not scared,' Kelly said, lifting her chin. 'I just want to build up a buffer before we move, a little nest egg that I can rely on in case…'

The room went very quiet. After a few seconds Chloe leaned over and put her hand on top of Kelly's. 'In case it comes back,' she said softly.

Kelly swallowed and nodded. 'I need to know I won't lose the house if I can't work for a while. The boys shouldn't have to go through that all over again.'

There was the sound of keys in the front door and the tiny stampede happened all over again, except this time Cal and Ben were shouting, 'Uncle Dan! Uncle Dan!'

Chloe stood up. 'Okay, I'll stop pushing. It's just that I can't help but feel that you're marking time, and that's not you. You're such a go-getter and I can't understand why you don't want to *go get* the house of your dreams—' she lowered her voice '—or a gorgeous man who's into you.'

Kelly stood up too. Of course Chloe didn't get it. She hadn't lost the home she'd thought she'd stay in till she died, the house that both Cal and Ben had been born in. She hadn't watched the man she loved walk away without a backward glance and then take every opportunity to grind her even further into the dirt with the heel of his shoe. She hadn't watched her children sleeping and felt sick with fear that one day she wouldn't be there to tuck them in at night.

'I'll go and ask Dan if he'll give you a lift home,' Chloe said, heading for the hallway. 'Save you getting the bus.'

Kelly nodded but her sister-in-law was no longer in the room to see it. She put her half-drunk wine down and picked up her handbag.

She knew she needed to get past those things, she really did. But it was easier said than done. That was why getting the house was important.

She allowed herself a moment to linger on Chloe's *other* suggestion of how to move on....

Okay, she admitted it. A hot fling with someone like Jason Knight would be fun. But she wasn't looking for fun. Didn't need it. That wasn't what her life was about at the moment. So she was going forward with her plans to save and buy a house because, once that was done, she knew she'd be able to stop holding her breath. She'd have taken the first step to moving on.

'Boys!' she yelled and headed towards the sitting room. 'Get your stuff together. We're going in five minutes!'

CHAPTER THREE

'KELLY, COULD I see you before you go this evening?'

Kelly stared at the closed office door and then the clock. Half past four. She'd hoped she'd be able to slip away quietly, with a polite farewell and a nod, as she'd done all week. This was the last thing she needed on a Friday afternoon. Especially *this* Friday afternoon. She was physically and mentally exhausted. They'd worked hard on the multimedia presentation Jason was putting together for Dale McGrath's camp all week, and her boss had certainly flung everything at it—a slide show, a brochure, a promo video.

She was also tired because she'd discovered Jason did everything at one speed: fast forward. And Jason's bounce seemed to be contagious. She'd accomplished more in a week than she ever could have imagined. More than she'd have managed in a month not long ago. But that didn't mean she wasn't dog tired at this end of the week.

To make it worse, he was so blooming enthusiastic! Instead of seeing the extra workload as an inconvenience, something to be got through to get to the end goal, Jason was like a big kid with a new toy. How could they make the promo video more interesting, slicker, glitzier? Could the video guy put in that cool fade he'd just shown them? Kelly could still see the big grin that had spread across Jason's face when the technician had done just that. Most disconcerting.

The other reason Kelly was exhausted was because she was doing her level best not to like her new boss. Not that she wanted to *dislike* him; she just wanted to stay professionally neutral, but that was very difficult when he kept wearing the same expression her boys did when they knew it was Saturday morning and they were going out to play football.

She rose from her seat, blew out a breath as she picked up her notepad and pen and then opened Jason's door.

She chickened out of direct eye contact for a few seconds, leaving it until she was pulling out the chair opposite his desk and sitting in it, giving herself a few seconds in which to prepare for the inevitable kick in the ribcage when she looked at him.

It still came when she looked up, winding her more thoroughly than usual—maybe because, instead of the usual glimmer of both humour and challenge in his eyes, he was looking far too serious.

But, unfortunately, Kelly discovered she liked serious from him. The way his brows drew together and his focus hardened just made her pulse drum all the harder.

Oh, help. If he kept this up she'd be toast. And she'd done so well burying Chloe's stupid suggestion about a hot and heavy rebound fling.

She cleared her throat. 'Is there something wrong?'

Jason stared at her for a minute then swivelled his laptop round to face her. The promo video they'd been working on began to play, not the first rough cut she'd already seen, but a more polished version. It ran for a couple of minutes and she watched the now familiar footage roll past, feeling Jason's eyes on her the whole time. When it finished he just said, 'Well?'

Kelly frowned. 'I think it looks great,' she said. 'Especially the tidied up graphics.' It was unlike any running shoe ad she'd ever seen. Instead of concentrating on lone runners pounding along through mountainous scenery or busy city streets, it was full of fast-paced shots of all sorts of things. Interesting things, colourful things, vibrant things. The clip left her feeling energised and ready to zing along the corridor at speed. That had been Jason's idea: to convey the swiftness of Mercury, without even showing a runner or a shoe.

She stopped staring at the blank laptop screen and met his gaze. 'If there's something the matter with it, I can't see it.'

She didn't get it. All week Jason had been banging on about how it had needed to be slicker, hipper...cooler. The finished product looked all of that and more.

He turned the laptop back to face himself, fiddled with the mouse, and when he turned it round again a section of the video swooping through the skyscrapers of Manhattan began to play.

'What are those graphics running underneath?' he asked in a low tone. 'I didn't authorise those.'

Kelly's mouth opened and closed. 'Those were

the stats you wanted to include, that we were waiting for from Research and Design. When I gave your last feedback to the production company they'd just come in, so I asked the team to find a way to add them in.'

Instead of looking pleased at her efficiency, which he'd been complimenting her on all week, Jason continued to look at her with unblinking eyes. 'Without consulting me?'

Kelly swallowed. He'd been very busy on an international call at the time, and she'd known he'd wanted to get the notes off to the production company as soon as possible. 'I thought that was what you wanted.'

Jason flipped the laptop closed and pushed it to one side before leaning back in his office chair. 'I decided to keep the facts and figures to the brochure, just let the video represent the ethos and aspirational qualities of the product—which you would have known, if you'd taken the time to ask me.'

Oh.

Jason sighed. 'I know I said I like your initiative, Kelly, but you've been here less than a week and you're already starting to make executive decisions.'

Kelly looked at her hands folded in her lap. 'I'm sorry,' she said, and she probably should have left it there, but somehow the truth came barrelling out of her mouth anyway. 'To be honest, I didn't think you'd mind. I thought you'd just…forgotten.'

Jason's eyebrows rose. 'So now you're telling me that I can't do my job properly and that a temp who's been here five days needs to pick up after me?'

Okay, it sounded bad when he put it that way.

Jason shook his head and looked away. 'You didn't think I'd care,' he said wearily. 'But why would I *not* care when the new product I've been working on for close to two years is on the line?'

Thankfully, she managed to swallow her next response. *Because you don't seem to care about anything too deeply,* she'd almost said. *Because everything seems like one big game to you.* Just like her boys, he only seemed to care about how edgy or flashy or cool everything was.

'I'm sorry,' she said again, but this time there was an added ring of sincerity to her tone. 'It's nothing to do with you, really. It's me.…'

Okay…this was starting to sound like a bad break-up.

'Sometimes I'm a little too independent,' she added. 'It's just that recently I've had to… I've been used to…'

Making it worse, Kelly. He doesn't want to hear about your personal woes.

She took a moment then continued. 'I'll contact Ace Productions right away and ask them to take it out.'

Jason's expression softened. 'No. Leave it. Your instinct was good. But it's my project and I get the final say. Just because I'm enthusiastic about my work doesn't mean I take it lightly.'

She nodded. She hadn't known that about him. And now she did. Good. She let out the breath she'd been holding and her lips started to curve.

Jason regarded Kelly with interest. All week he'd been charming and friendly to her—as charming as he could be without actually *flirting*—but he hadn't had more than a nod or an affirmative phrase. And now he'd just told her off and she was smiling at him? How did that work?

He smiled back. Not his charm-the-birds-from-the-trees smile, just an ordinary one. A weary one.

It had been a long week. 'Okay. Well, as long as that's clear. This project is my baby. And I feel exactly the same way about it as a mother feels about her children.'

She squinted at him slightly, as if she wasn't quite sure it was possible to equate a running shoe with a living, breathing mini human being. 'If you say so….'

Jason's smile upgraded to a grin. He didn't know why he liked his prickly assistant's prickles so much, but he did.

'I know you're not going to believe me, but in a creative sense it really is like seeing something born. Years ago now, I had the seed of an idea, just the inkling of a new design that might really improve a running shoe, and it's been growing and developing ever since. The shoe is finished—it's ready to go out into the big wide world—and I want the very best for it.'

'Why?' she said, looking back at him. The expression she wore was of open curiosity, not guarded politeness, as he'd been used to from her all week.

'Why does anybody want the best for their "babies"?'

She pressed her lips together and thought for a while. 'Because you want them to fulfil their potential—be all they can be.'

He nodded. 'Exactly. And I know these shoes have the potential to be revolutionary—I just need to convince the rest of the world of that too.'

'Why Dale McGrath? You said the preliminary approach you made wasn't received with much interest. Why not just target someone else, someone who can catch your vision?'

He put his hands behind his head and let his weight push his chair into recline so he could stare at the ceiling. Why *did* he want McGrath so badly? There were plenty of other sportsmen out there. Some who were showier, more charismatic. But Dale's was the face he had seen when he'd imagined the first ad campaign and now he couldn't shake it. 'I don't know why, but he just fits. Call it gut instinct.'

With that he sat up and his chair sprung upright behind him. The clock on the opposite wall said it was close to five.

Kelly followed his gaze and started to stand up. 'Well, if that's all,' she said calmly, 'I really should be going.'

He planted his feet on the floor and rose too. 'Time for a quick drink? There's a great little place just round the corner.'

Kelly froze. 'I don't think so,' she said as she straightened and met his eyes.

'Not a date,' he added quickly. 'Just to celebrate an intense but productive first week. Purely professional.'

She looked at him suspiciously.

'Look,' he said, 'half the Aspire team will be in there anyway. It's a regular Friday-night hang-out.'

She shook her head. 'I'm sorry, I can't.'

'Can't or won't?'

'Can't,' she said stiffly. All that armour plating that had melted away when he'd been telling her about Mercury was back up in full force. 'There's somewhere I need to be.'

One corner of his mouth hitched up. 'Can't you make him wait? Just for half an hour?'

She hugged her notepad to her chest. 'Actually, there's more than one and, no, they can't wait.'

Two? Whoa. When he'd labelled her as a wild-cat he'd only got it half right.

'My sons,' she said quickly, then stared him down.

Jason stared back. He knew what this was about.

She was expecting a reaction from him. He disappointed her by *not* running screaming from the room. So she was a mom. Didn't bother him any.

Except if...

'You're married?' They'd been in close proximity all week. Surely he'd have noticed it before now. A ring was the first thing he looked for when an attractive woman walked across his path.

Okay, maybe not the *first* thing. But it was definitely in the top five.

He hadn't thought it was possible for her to look any more poker-like, but she surprised him yet again. 'No, I'm not married.'

No problem, then.

But Kelly didn't look as if she shared his opinion.

She'd wanted to fudge it. He could tell it by the way her lips had moved silently before she'd said no. But she hadn't. And she could have invented a fictional Mr Bradford and been on her way home in a flash if she'd wanted to. That was a sign, right there. One he should probably not be paying attention to, but it was a hard habit to break.

'After-work drinks... Not a good idea. It's against the no-dating-at-work policy,' she said matter-of-factly.

Jason frowned. 'We don't have a no-dating policy.' He should know. He'd ditched it so he could start dating his former PA. They'd turned out to be such a good team. In the office… Out of the office… Especially in the bedroom. But then she'd gone and got all serious on him, talking about moving in together and hosting dinner parties. Jason shuddered. It had ended with a nuclear fight, a cold space in his bed and a vacancy at the office. That had been two months ago, and they hadn't found anyone suitable to replace her long-term yet. In the office, of course. Out of the office Jason wasn't looking for anything more than 'temporary'.

'You might not have a no-dating policy, but I do,' Kelly said quite seriously.

Jason blinked. Had he just heard her right? It took him a few moments to gather a sensible reply. 'I said it wasn't a date. Just socialising after work.'

She narrowed her eyes. 'Socialising is fine, and I'd be quite happy to go out in a group, but not tonight, and not alone with you.' She smiled sweetly at him. 'Have a good weekend, Mr Knight.' And then she was gone. Out of the office and down the corridor before he could think of anything else to say.

Jason let out a dry, self-mocking laugh. Well, that told him! He didn't get that response very often when he asked a woman out for a drink. Far from it.

He sat back down in his chair and rubbed his face with his hand.

Oh, Kelly Bradford might *say* she didn't want to go out with him, but all week he'd seen the way she'd looked at him when she thought he hadn't been watching. That was why he'd issued his invitation in the first place. For a woman who told the bald, unvarnished truth about everything else, she was lying about this.

How intriguing.

And how very tantalising. He laughed again, but it was a lighter, more joyous noise this time.

Love-one to Ms Bradford. But that didn't mean she'd won the match.

CHAPTER FOUR

JASON STARED AT the email he'd just read a few seconds longer then closed the window down with a grunt of exasperation. What had he expected? That suddenly the world would take the rich kid playing with his daddy's company seriously, even though he'd spent years turning it around?

The rules in this game were stacked against him. Just because his ancestors had been successful and he'd been born into a wealthy family, he couldn't be seen as just another businessman with a revolutionary idea to sell. He couldn't even be applauded as a man trying to rebuild his life after a career-ending injury. No, the world had decided he, with the help of his blue-blood friends, had brought misfortune on himself and it had no sympathy for him. He'd been branded with that assessment and no one was ever going to let him forget it.

Certainly not Dale McGrath.

His team had sent a polite refusal: Dale, unfortunately, did not have time in his schedule to see Jason while he was in London next week. The wording had made it all seem very benign, but Jason knew the sound of a door slamming shut when he heard it.

Oh, he could still get a good name to endorse the shoes, but it wouldn't be the same. With the fastest man on the planet in his campaign, they could have seen Mercury go stellar. Dale McGrath was the best, and Jason wanted the best. Anything less was just second place.

Kelly knocked on his door at that moment. He recognised her sharp, clean rap instantly and yelled for her to come in. As she approached his desk, she frowned, and then she stopped walking. 'You heard?' she asked nervously. 'What did they say?'

Jason picked up his baby basketball, took his time lining it up perfectly then sunk it through the hoop. He was getting very good at office basketball, so at least that was *one* thing he was excelling at.

'He said no.'

They both watched the ball speed across the carpet and roll to a stop against the wall. He didn't go and retrieve it.

'Oh, Jason! I'm so sorry. I know how hard you've been working on this.'

He spun round to look at her, ambushed by the first bit of non-confrontational sincerity he'd heard from her in the month she'd been working for him, but his mouth remained a grim line. 'Don't sweat it,' he said, then picked up his cellphone and fiddled with a few buttons. Which buttons he wasn't exactly sure, because he wasn't really paying attention. He just didn't want to see that look of empathy or pity or whatever it was in her eyes. Better just to pretend it didn't matter. But, unlike other times, when he'd just been able to flick a switch and flush the bad feeling away, this one hung around.

It loomed over him like a dark cloud all day—while he listened to Kelly's update on the ad campaign for their new range of trampolines. While he sat through meeting after meeting. By four o'clock he was ready to punch something and that was not a good state to be in.

He knew those kinds of adrenalin rushes only led to shows of macho stupidity—a release mechanism of his—and the last time he'd let something

burrow this deep he'd managed to ruin two people's lives.

The only way Jason knew how to stop feeling
like a loser in one arena was to win in another,
even if it was just a game of checkers or jacks. He
wondered if Kelly knew how to play jacks, if she
would mind kneeling down on the carpet and indulging him.

Just the thought of that black skirt tightening
over her butt as she leaned forward to catch the
little ball, lip caught under her teeth in concentra-
tion, made his insides shiver.

Maybe there was something *better* than jacks....

Maybe it was time he and Kelly stopped deny-
ing the obvious electricity that arced between them
whenever they shared a room. Winning her over
could feel a lot like winning, period.

Oh, he knew what he'd promised Julie, but desperate times called for desperate measures. He
needed to let off some steam before he did something really dumb.

But he guessed a direct play would only bomb
out. She'd scurry away back into that hard shell
she hid behind most of the time. As it was, he only

got tiny glimpses of the softer, warmer woman underneath.

Just as well his grandfather had taught Jason to play chess from the time he was old enough to hold a piece in his chubby fingers and not shove it in his mouth. He knew how to plan and project. He knew how to move and counter move. And now he was going to use all that skill on his temporary PA, until she cracked and was as unflinchingly honest about the attraction humming between them as she was about everything else.

At the end of that afternoon Kelly looked up from her desk and saw a trio of female Aspire employees hanging around in the corridor.

'Hey, Kelly. You coming across the road to Joey's for a bit?'

The one who'd spoken was the junior member of staff she'd met on that fateful day in the Human Resources office. Of course, she now knew the girl's name was Chantelle. She was about to make an excuse and head off home, but she didn't get any further than opening her mouth.

Chloe was looking after the boys again this evening and she'd actively encouraged Kelly to go out for an after-work drink. Especially when she'd discovered Jason had asked Kelly out at the end of her first week. Of course, this was nothing to do with Jason, but what Chloe didn't know wouldn't hurt her.

She smiled back at the three women. 'Actually, I'd really like that. Just give me two seconds.'

Before collecting her handbag from under the desk, she rapped on the office door and stuck her head in. 'I'm going now, Jason.'

He was deep in some paperwork on his desk. He hardly looked up, just grunted an offhand farewell. Kelly inhaled and closed the door again. He hadn't tried asking her out again since that first Friday, and that was good. That was what she wanted. It was just…

Well, no woman liked to think her allure had evaporated. She sighed. Well, that was what you got for having a big mouth. She tended to blow the cobwebs out of most subjects she touched, so she shouldn't really be surprised if Jason had found it a turn-off. Tim certainly had towards the end of their marriage.

Okay, she thought, as she collected her belongings and headed for the lifts with the group of gossiping girls. Jason might not appreciate her bull-in-a-china-shop approach to male/female relationships, but she knew it was working just fine in their professional pairing. He'd told her it was refreshing to have someone who didn't just parrot the word 'yes' at him. He didn't always follow her suggestions, but he listened, and that was what counted. She felt part of a team working for him, not just a skivvy to be ordered around and sent to make coffee.

Careful, Kelly. Any minute now you'll be admitting you like the guy, and that's far too dangerous.

Professional. Yes, that was what she'd told him she wanted out of their relationship, and he'd stuck to it. He'd respected her wishes. And maybe she could like him just a little bit for that. A *very* little bit.

Joey's was busy with familiar faces from Aspire when Kelly followed Chantelle and her two friends through the door. A very chivalrous lad from Accounting cleared off a stool and offered it to her. She smiled and said thank you and hopped on top of it. Chantelle ordered cocktails—her treat, she said—and Kelly gratefully accepted hers when it arrived. After the last couple of weeks, she really needed it.

And, as the minutes ticked on and she joined in a conversation about what was going on in a popular soap opera, she began to feel the tension ebb from her shoulders. Just for a while she was the Kelly she vaguely remembered being, once upon a time. Not somebody's mother. Not somebody's harried ex-wife. Not a single parent carrying the weight of the world on her shoulders. Just Kelly. It was quite liberating.

In the middle of a discussion about the latest line up of hopefuls for the current TV talent show, she saw Chantelle look in the direction of the door and smile a secret little smile. Kelly was as nosey as she was blunt, so she turned to see who had just walked in.

Crap.

She whipped her head back round again and concentrated on her half-drunk cosmopolitan.

Jason. She should have guessed he'd turn up sooner or later. Chloe *would* be pleased.

But the bar was crowded, she reasoned, and there were plenty of Aspire employees ready to kiss up to the boss. There was no reason she would even have to talk to him. She would just carry on chatting to the girls and try not to be aware of where he was. Difficult, though, when her skin prickled every time he came within ten feet of her.

There it went again. She picked up her glass and took a great gulp while trying to radiate silent messages: *I'm not here…. Go and find someone else to talk to…. There are much more interesting people on the other side of the room….*

'I wouldn't have picked you for a cocktail kind of girl,' a deep voice said from over her left shoulder. Kelly downed the remainder, just to make a point. She tried to pretend she hadn't heard him, but the guy sitting next to her offered Jason his stool and Jason slid into her peripheral vision. Poop. Kelly's skin prickled so hard she had to stop herself scratching. At work, she had the added help of a big, sturdy desk between them. Here in the bar, with the lighting low, the hum of conversation around them and the scent of his aftershave filling her nostrils, it was hard to ignore the crazy attraction she had for him.

At least he was just being friendly, she tried to kid herself. At least her allure had worn off.

But when she turned to greet him, the flicker

of heat in his eyes contradicted her. Kelly felt her legs wobble on the stool.

'Oh, I'm a cocktail girl all right,' she said, lying through her teeth. 'Have them for breakfast, lunch and dinner.'

Jason nodded seriously. 'So *that's* what you keep in that insulated coffee cup on your desk. I had wondered.'

Damn him. Now she wanted to smile.

'Peach daiquiri today,' she said. 'Most refreshing.'

Jason laughed, and Kelly felt her lips tugging up at the corners.

'Okay, you're right,' she said wearily. 'I like them, but cocktails aren't usually my thing. I prefer my drinks one at a time, not all mixed together.'

'Like…?'

She shrugged. 'I like a good red wine…' She tipped her head to one side and thought for a minute. 'But I think my absolute favourite is a cold beer straight from the bottle on a warm summer's evening.'

Jason looked at her empty glass then nodded at the barman. 'Let me get you one.'

Kelly shook her head vehemently. 'No. I pay for my own drinks.'

'Didn't Chantelle buy you that one?' And he nodded in the direction of the girls she'd come with, all with matching drinks.

'That's not the same and you know it.'

'So not accepting drinks from men is also part of your no-dating-at-work policy?'

She nodded. It seemed like a good time to include that clause.

'The same way you don't want to go out after work with me, but you don't mind going out in a group?'

'Ye-es,' she said slowly, feeling that somehow this was a trick question. She saw him nod a greeting at someone, and the look he gave was also a little conspiratorial. She whipped her head round to see who he was looking at and found Chantelle smiling back at him, toasting him with her cocktail glass. Kelly turned to study her boss again.

Had he…had he set this up? Had he asked Chantelle to bring her down here? Surely not. She looked at her still-empty glass. Who knew that a bit of vodka and cranberry could make you so paranoid?

'So groups are okay?' Jason said from beside her.

'Huh?' Kelly frowned and looked up at him. This evening was getting increasingly surreal.

Jason waved at the barman and leaned over to shout something in his ear. The man straightened and yelled out, 'Next round's on the boss!'

The crowd roared its appreciation and there was a stampede to the bar. Kelly glared at Jason as best she could past the people who had squeezed between their two stools to wave at the bar staff.

Technically, she'd won. He hadn't bought her a drink—at least, not just her—but the satisfied smirk on his face made her feel as if she'd just been trumped.

She wasn't sure if she liked that, but he'd had a rough day. McGrath's refusal had been a disappointment, and maybe teasing her now that they were out of the office was his way of blowing off steam. She decided to give him the benefit of the doubt.

She ordered a second cosmo. Beer seemed too… chummy. Cocktails were suitably aloof. As she sipped it she tried hard to remain equally aloof and detached from her boss.

It didn't work very well. She kept forgetting and

getting absorbed in a funny story he was telling the people gathered around them, and then she'd start laughing and smiling. That in itself wasn't *so* bad, but then she'd catch Jason's eye and discover it held a twinkle just for her.

What was worse, she liked it. Liked feeling as if they were a unit of two amidst the larger group of Aspire employees. Co-conspirators, even.

But soon she began to wonder *why* he was on such top form that evening. Wasn't he disappointed too? She searched for signs of it, but when someone asked him directly about the McGrath deal, he just batted the subject away, as he would a pesky fly, telling the person who'd asked that it was no big deal.

That was when Kelly started to get angry with him.

She'd worked really, really hard on that project, had become invested in it emotionally, because she'd *believed* in the shoes. She'd *believed* in Jason Knight and his passion for them.

Once again she'd been suckered in by a good-looking man with a line. Because now he was laughing it all off as if it didn't matter.

It started to boil inside her as she nursed the last

dregs of her cocktail. Perhaps this was how he was… Tim had been a bit like that, suffering from sudden and overpowering passions for hobbies or pet projects or even TV programmes. Golf had lasted a year. After he'd spent a fortune on getting top of the range kit, of course. Squash had been next. Then paintball. And they hadn't been able to watch one episode of a favourite TV show a week, like normal people. Tim had been all about the DVD box set—multiple episodes per evening until her head had spun with the plot lines and characters and she'd ended up dreaming about them all night.

So, it didn't matter how good Jason Knight's broad shoulders looked in his immaculately cut suit. She didn't need to get enamoured with another man like that. A man who couldn't commit to something for more than a couple of weeks. She'd bet he had a set of clubs mouldering in his hall cupboard too.

So she downed the last of her cosmo and slammed her empty glass on the bar, then she stood up, said a terse goodbye to the group and pushed her way through the crowd to the door.

The delicious air of a spring evening wrapped

itself around her as she stepped outside, cooling her skin and sharpening her senses. Sharpening her anger too. The echo of her heels on the paving slabs bounced off the walls of a low bridge as she passed under it and marched down the road to the Tube station.

Jason looked in both directions when he burst from the door of Joey's and quickly spotted his PA marching off down the street as if she was on her way to execute something. Or some*one*.

'Kelly!' he called out, but those legs just kept striding. 'Hey, Kelly!'

She didn't slow or stop, but there was a slight straightening of her spine that indicated she'd heard him just fine. He smiled to himself. He could play it that way, if that was what she wanted.

Kelly's legs might be long, but his were longer and her stride was hampered by both heels and a skirt. It wasn't long before he caught up and fell into step beside her. She didn't look at him.

'Is something up?' he asked. 'Did I do something to make you mad?'

He didn't get it. He thought he'd been a great guy this evening, but when she kept her focus on the brightly lit Tube sign a little farther along the street he knew his gut was right. She was mad. Now he just had to find out why.

Most women would have iced him out, punctuating the silence with only a few choice phrases designed to make him quit and go back to the bar. But Kelly Bradford wasn't most women.

She tried, he could tell, but he almost heard the snap in her resolve as she turned to him and opened her mouth.

'Typical man,' she muttered. 'The world revolves around you, doesn't it? It has to be all about you.'

'No,' he said too quickly—and maybe a little defensively.

'Maybe I just need to get home to my boys,' she added. 'Maybe there's more to my life than propping up a bar and making everyone think I'm God's gift by cracking jokes and flashing my wallet around.'

She *was* mad at him! He knew it!

'Kelly…are you saying that the only reason you're sprinting down this street is because you need to catch a train? That's what all this is about?'

'Exactly,' she said, and smirked to herself.

Jason smothered his own urge to smile. 'Then why have you just walked right past the station?'

Kelly let out a short pithy word, turned on her heel and headed back in the other direction. Jason took a moment to enjoy his little victory, smiling at her back as she stalked away from him, and then he began to jog lightly to catch her up.

But as he reached her his smile faded. He gently reached for her wrist. She pulled it away before he made contact, but at least she stopped and faced him instead of walking on.

He needed to know. He needed to know what was driving her nuts. Him, yeah, but it was more than that, and suddenly finding out what was becoming inexplicably important. 'This isn't just about getting home for bath time,' he said.

Kelly's jaw tensed and she shot him a guilty look. No poker face at all, this one.

'You said those shoes were your baby,' she said, accusation rich in her tone.

He nodded. Yeah, he had said that. So what?

'Well, your *baby* is lying critically ill in hospital while you're living it up down at the pub, celebrating.'

He found his blood pressure rising to match hers.

'So I decided to cheer myself up a little. Hardly a crime! But it's *my* project that's been knocked back, *my* dream lying in the gutter. Who gave you the right to judge? Why should you care?'

Okay, he should pay attention to that throbbing feeling in his temples. It was when he got this way that he did dumb things. Things he regretted. Usually things other people regretted too. But Kelly had a way of making the adrenalin course through his veins, despite all his best efforts to keep it locked away.

She put her hands on her hips, glared at him with glistening eyes. 'Because you made me care, damn you!'

Her words were like a slap. That couldn't be right. Nobody cared about the things he cared about. Because all he cared about was having a good time and messing up other people's lives, apparently. Now the adrenalin was pumping harder, faster, but it brought with it a chill he recognised, a chill he didn't care for, and he realised he couldn't *let* Kelly care. Because if she cared, he would care, and that was something he really didn't want to do. He'd better do something about that fast. Something to make her not care. Something to make her believe he was exactly who she thought he was.

He didn't even think about his next move; he just did it. He looked down at her shining eyes and her full lips, and the next second his arms closed around her and he was tasting those lips. She went rigid, and somewhere in the back of Jason's brain a thought knocked to be let in. A thought that maybe this was the *dumbness* talking and maybe this wasn't such a good idea after all.

For the first time in his life, he was on the verge of stepping back and apologising for kissing an attractive woman.

And he might have done too, if not for the fact that she started to kiss him back.

CHAPTER FIVE

SOMETHING INSIDE KELLY'S head was screaming at her, tugging at her frantically, telling her to pull away, have a little dignity. She slapped whatever it was into silence by snaking her arms around Jason's neck and pulling him closer.

Oh, she'd forgotten just how *good* this could be. Just how simple and uncomplicated and wonderful a first kiss could be.

It had been more than a decade since she'd had one of those. And, in the interim, kissing had turned from blissful and passionate to comfortable and familiar and finally to infrequent and guilt ridden. On Tim's part, anyway. At the time she hadn't known why he'd avoided her touch. In her darker moments she'd thought he'd been put off by the thought of kissing a woman who'd just been diagnosed with cancer.

But this—she sighed against his lips—this was perfect.

Then a chink of reality invaded her lovely warm haze.

This was also her boss. Wonderful as it might be, this was definitely not 'simple and uncomplicated'.

He'd shocked her, though. The moment she'd responded to him he'd stilled, as if he was surprised. Odd, when he'd been the one to initiate the kiss, when surely that was what he'd been slowly building up to all evening. The stillness hadn't lasted long, however. Moments later he'd pulled her to him and shown her just how high and how hot the flames of their insane chemistry could burn. She was surprised the illuminated Tube sign above their heads hadn't exploded in a shower of sparks.

The kiss quickly deepened into something more primal—and far less decent. If they kept this up, they were in danger of getting arrested.

It seemed Jason had come to the same conclusion because he pulled away. 'Which way is home?' he whispered in a husky voice that sent shivers down her spine.

That was the logical conclusion to what they'd just started, she knew. They'd gone *way* beyond a polite, end-of-a-first-date kiss, even though they'd skipped the date and gone straight for the lip action. But suddenly that *wonderful* something she'd been feeling congealed and became much more cold and slimy.

She couldn't take this guy home with her! What was she thinking?

More importantly, what was *he* thinking?

Scratch that. She knew exactly what Jason was thinking, and she needed to put him straight fast. She unhooked her hands from around his neck and dragged herself from him, backing away a few steps to put some distance between them. Maybe she should have felt better to see that, far from being slick and in control, he seemed to be just as disoriented as she was, but she didn't. She didn't want to feel any kind of sympathy for him at this moment. She needed to be angry with him. Because if she was angry with Jason, she couldn't be angry at herself for being so weak and stupid.

'We're not doing this,' she told him shakily.

Jason just looked a little confused.

'I told you it was a bad idea,' she reminded him. 'Against my personal policy—and it really should be against yours too!'

'I remember what you said,' he replied, 'but that

was *before* you were on the verge of ripping my shirt open. I kinda guessed you'd had a rethink on those rules of yours.'

Thinking hadn't been any part of the equation, unfortunately. But, now her brain had kicked in again, it felt very much the same as it always had done on the subject of Jason Knight and an illicit office fling.

'I'm not going to be your consolation prize for losing the McGrath deal,' she told him. 'Hot, angry sex with me will not solve anything.'

The look on Jason's face said he begged to differ. And Kelly was regretting her choice of words too. They'd conjured up all sorts of images that really weren't helping her sudden attack of self-control.

'I don't know…' he began, regaining some of his usual swagger.

That helped. Seeing him almost vulnerable after he'd broken their kiss had not. But now he was looking more like his usual self and that helped her remember who Jason Knight really was.

'Everything's a game to you, isn't it?' she said, shaking her head. 'What would this have been? Another point on your scoreboard? Another notch on your impressive bedpost?'

One corner of Jason's mouth hitched up. 'My bedpost *is* rather impressive,' he said with a bit of a drawl. Kelly ignored him. She stoked the returning anger until it was good and hot. He was proving her point nicely for her.

'Well, some of us don't have the luxury of playing life like it's a game,' she told him. 'You, with your nice suits and your flashy car and your big-money family... Of *course* nothing can touch you! But sometimes...' she felt her lip wobble and willed it to hold '...sometimes things happen that make you take life seriously. Very seriously.'

Jason stopped smiling. He gave her a look similar to the one he'd worn when he'd called her into his office about the video. Kelly's knees began to soften. She braced them back hard and looked him straight in the eye, daring him.

'You're saying that because my family has money nothing bad can ever happen to me?' he asked in a deceptively flat tone.

No, she hadn't meant it that way. She tried to explain further. 'I'm just saying that you mess around when you could do so much more, that money allows you to get away with that when the rest of us have no such buffer.'

His gaze had turned cold and she did her best not to shiver. 'So why didn't my daddy's money stop me messing up my shoulder? Why didn't it stop my brother ending up in a wheelchair? Tell me that, Kelly.'

She swallowed. Okay, she might have heard that about him in the past, but she'd forgotten all about those distant *Celebrity Life* articles when she'd been good and angry. There was one thing she did remember, though....

'The newspapers said that was your fault. They said you caused the accident that crippled your brother.' And she regretted those words the moment they left her lips. She always joked she wished someone would invent a filter that would fit between brain and mouth, and now she wished that not only were there such a device, but that she'd invested in the best money could buy.

The colour drained from Jason's face and he stared at her.

'You're right,' he said. 'Hot, angry sex with you *would* be a really bad idea. In fact, any kind of sex with you would be a bad idea.' And then he turned and walked back in the direction of the bar.

* * *

Kelly wasn't usually one for attacks of conscience, but hers niggled her all weekend. Okay, it didn't just niggle. It shouted. It berated. It condemned. By Monday morning she was feeling bruised and sore. The last thing she wanted to do was to go and face Jason, but she arrived early, aiming to catch him while the building was quiet.

She hurried into the building, pressed the button for the lift at least three times and then tapped her foot as it climbed higher and higher. Moments later she was standing outside his office door, listening to the telltale thump of that stupid basketball. She straightened her blouse, took a deep breath and knocked.

'Come in.' The voice was flat and expressionless. Did he know it was her?

She pushed the door open and leaned her head inside. 'Is now a good time? Because I can come back later if it's more convenient. I don't want to disturb you, so I'll—'

She was cut off by Jason's short, sharp laugh. 'You don't want to *disturb* me?'

He sounded incredulous. Sarcastic. That wasn't good. Secretly she'd been hoping that over the weekend he'd turned back into the good old Jason who drove her crazy, who let anything negative roll off him. Unfortunately, the silent, surly, unsmiling Jason was still in residence.

She stepped into the office and closed the door behind her, keeping her hands on the handle and her backside pressed against them. She opened her mouth but no words came. Jason cocked an eyebrow, apparently amused at her speechlessness. She swallowed and cleared her throat.

'I'm sorry,' she said a little hoarsely. 'About what I said on Friday night. I overstepped the mark.'

He stared back at her.

'I…I shouldn't have flung stupid gossip back at you. I know nothing about it—'

'Seems you know all there is to know,' Jason said, and spun his chair round to face the floor-to-ceiling windows on the other side of the office. 'You were right. It was my fault my brother ended up in a wheelchair.'

Kelly discovered that while she was very good at dishing out the harsh truth, she hadn't really had that much experience of being on the receiving end—unless you counted Dan, which she didn't, because who ever listened to their brother?

She was scared. Scared of what to say, what to do next. Was this how other people felt when she unleashed her tongue on them? Was this what the stunned silence after one of her outbursts meant? She wanted to run out of the room and pretend this conversation hadn't started, but she couldn't. She wasn't a coward. She reminded herself she'd stared cancer in the face and won, so surely she could do this.

She walked over to the bookcase where there was a picture of Jason with two other men. One was older and looked like a sterner, leaner version of her boss. He and Jason were both standing behind the other man, who was seated in a wheelchair. His features were different from Jason's and his hair was a sandy blond, but she could tell this was his brother. There was something about the determination behind those eyes…. In the picture, Jason's brother was wearing a sporting uniform and he had a large gold medal round his neck.

'What's his event?' she asked, and she heard Jason's chair creak as he turned to see what she was doing.

'Swimming,' he said, just a hint of surprise in his voice.

'Like you.'

Jason snorted. 'Not like me. Brad's got the medals and I haven't—and he does it without the use of his legs.' He met her gaze. 'Go on. Tell me how uncharitable I am. Tell me how childish I am to talk like that.'

Kelly swallowed. She'd heard the bitterness in his voice. She knew all about sibling rivalry. With two thick-headed brothers to contend with, she'd had to grow up fighting, but the emptiness in Jason's eyes spoke of something more. She looked at the picture again—how the older man's hand rested comfortably on Brad's shoulder, how Jason seemed as if he'd been slotted in afterwards, as if he could easily have been airbrushed out and the balance of the composition wouldn't have been upset in any way.

'I don't think you're childish,' she said. 'I think you might have a chip on your shoulder the size of the Empire State Building, but I don't think you're childish.'

Jason's features softened from anger into surprise. 'Really?'

Kelly let out a dry laugh. 'When have you ever known me to lie?'

For once, Jason didn't have a smart remark or a joke to fend off the silence. He looked like a little boy who'd been punished for something he hadn't done and then finally told he was off the hook. It made Kelly's heart contract in a way she didn't welcome. She didn't want him to remind her of her boys. It was bad enough to be attracted to this man; she didn't want to feel protective of him too.

'For what it's worth, I really am sorry,' she said, putting the picture back on the shelf and walking towards him. She glanced back at the frame. 'If it bothers you so much, why do you keep it there, staring you in the face all day long?'

Jason's mouth flattened into a grim line. 'To remind me.'

'Of what?' she asked softly.

He looked into her eyes. It was a shock. For the first time she felt she was seeing the real him—no gloss, no game playing. It made her feel a little bit wobbly. 'To keep me jealous. To make me want to drive forwards and prove myself.'

And to punish yourself, she thought. But she didn't say it.

And she got it now. Why the shoes were so important. Why he hadn't been able to bear admitting failure. Why he'd distracted himself with a good night out, shaking it off and pretending that nothing was wrong. And then she'd gone and shattered the insulated bubble he'd created for himself—and if anyone knew how important that bubble could be when tough times came, it was Kelly.

'I'll clean out my desk as soon as I get a box,' she told him. 'I just need to go and find one.'

Jason sat up in his chair. 'Don't.'

Kelly's mouth dropped open. 'But I... But you...'

He shrugged. 'I don't think my behaviour on Friday was saintly, either. I don't usually force myself on women.'

Kelly's shoulders sagged. 'You didn't. Not really.' She hated the next words that came out of her mouth. 'I mean, I was in it as much as you were.'

There was a flicker of amusement behind Jason's eyes.

'Doesn't mean I think it's a good idea to repeat the experience,' she added quickly. 'Far too complicated.'

He gave her a rueful look. 'I hate to admit it, but I think you're right.'

Kelly exhaled. That was good, wasn't it? That he agreed with her. She should be feeling pleased.

And she was. It was just that the morning had been a bit of an emotional roller coaster and the notion still hadn't caught up with her.

'We're agreed, then,' she said, and watched carefully for his reaction.

'I guess we are.'

She hadn't realised she'd been holding her breath until she released it in unison with him. 'What now?'

Jason looked up at her. 'We start again. There are plenty of other sports figures out there who'd love to endorse Mercury. We just have to find ourselves one and convince them of that.'

Kelly smiled at him. The old Jason wasn't back, but the snapping, snarling one had retreated into his cave. And she kind of liked this new one, the one who looked at her as an ally rather than something to be conquered.

He stood up and reached across the desk, offering her his hand. It was exactly the same gesture he'd made the first time they'd met, and she understood its significance. New beginnings, fresh starts…

Swallowing slightly, she reached over and slid her hand in his, and he gripped her fingers lightly.

They stayed like that for a few seconds, not moving, not shaking, but still cementing what they'd just verbally agreed. However, underneath that feeling of everything settling back into its proper order, her blood started to pulse harder, her nerve endings quivered and she couldn't quite ignore the steady thrum deep down in her core.

Unsettled, she pulled her hand away, not daring to look at him, then she turned and walked back to her desk, closing the office door behind her.

Don't be stupid, Kelly. It was just a handshake, that was all. Nothing to get dramatic about. Just a simple handshake.

She walked round her desk, dropped into her chair and stared at her blank computer monitor. They could do this, couldn't they? They could work together without sex getting in the way. *Couldn't they?*

Over the next couple of months they *did* manage to keep sex out of their relationship—on the surface, at least. And that was good enough for Kelly. It was always there, simmering away underneath, but she told herself she was getting used to it, like a dull toothache you put off going to the dentist about.

She didn't regret backing away from whatever had been brewing between them. Jason had spent the intervening time cementing her sense of self-righteousness on that front. While he obviously hadn't been dating anyone at work, he *had* been dating.

Kelly had a list on the notepad on her desk. A list of names. Girls' names.

When a new one called they'd sound breezy and hopeful. Kelly had now started adding to the list just based on a particular tone of voice on the other end of the line. But the women whose names were at the top of the list had lost that optimism now. If they called at all, they sounded tearful and stressed. More than one had shouted at her on the phone when she'd told them Jason wasn't there or was unavailable, thinking that Kelly was covering for him.

She hadn't been. If he wasn't busy she put them straight through. He could deal with them himself. Definitely *not* part of her job description.

One morning, Jason buzzed through and asked her to come into his office. Kelly rose from her desk and opened the door. The little kick of attraction still came as she spotted him bent over his desk, scribbling furiously on a pad, but she didn't dread or even resent it anymore. *You're alive,* it told her. She almost welcomed the daily reminder, even missed it on the weekends.

One day, maybe, she'd find a man who made her heart jump the same way, a man who was ready to be a grown-up about his relationships. One who wouldn't run when the going got tough. If there were such a fairy tale creature, of course….

Jason looked up as she crossed the office and sat down in the chair opposite him. She smiled gently as she met his gaze.

It wasn't this one. No, definitely not this one.

'Any updates?' he asked her.

She nodded and looked down at her notepad. 'Yes, all three runners have received the sample shoes. Emerson's out of the country at the moment, but the other two hope to test them out within the week and give us a verdict.'

'Good,' Jason said, nodding. 'I want to go to contract as soon as possible on this. We need to find us a face that fits.'

He made a little gesture with his mouth, pulling it down at the edges.

'What?' she asked.

He shrugged. 'Nothing.'

'Are you unhappy with any of the three we've shortlisted? Because we can keep looking...'

He shook his head. 'No. They're all...fine.' And then he started to tell her about the ideas he'd been discussing with the marketing department and the advertising company they'd hired. She scribbled away on her pad, noting down names and dates and times. Things for her to do and things to remind Jason of later, when the next amazing idea hit and he'd half forgotten about this one.

When their brief meeting came to an end, she rose to return to her desk.

'You're coming to the company picnic next Saturday, aren't you?' Jason asked. 'Bring your sons, there'll be plenty of other kids to play with.'

Kelly looked back at him. 'I think you're insane. This is London, not Los Angeles. Don't you know that organising something like that is practically an open invitation for the weather gods to come and mess with you?'

Jason leaned back in his chair and clasped his

hands behind his head. He dropped the tone of his voice and impersonated someone; his father, she guessed. 'The Knight Corporation is still a family company at heart, and the annual picnic is an important part of creating that ethos.'

She raised her eyebrows. 'Big fans of outdoor eating then, your family?'

He shrugged. 'Not really. Never once had one on the lawn at home, despite there being acres of it. Dad would never have been home for it anyway— too busy at the office. And my mother would never have thought to organise one without his say-so.' He gave her a tight smile. 'He let us go to the office picnic, though, so he could show what a great family man he was, so I can't complain.'

There was that hint of pain behind his laughing eyes again, the one she glimpsed every now and then that tugged at her heart. But Kelly had developed a coping mechanism for these moments, and it was very effective too. The key was to take a mental step back and see the big picture where Jason Knight was concerned, to remember that was only one facet of him and there were other things she needed to keep in the forefront of her consciousness.

She fumbled in her pocket for the tiny object she'd stowed there earlier. 'Erm…one of the cleaners gave this to me. She said she found it under your desk.'

She produced a gold hoop earring and placed it in front of him. Jason stared blankly at it.

So did Kelly. She hadn't been aware of another woman spending significant time in this office besides her these last few weeks. Somehow the knowledge made her feel…territorial.

He picked up the hoop and turned it over in his hand, frowning slightly.

Kelly let out an exasperated sigh and shook her head. 'You don't know who it belongs to, do you?'

The fact he didn't answer straight away told her all she needed to know, but then his eyes crinkled round the edges. 'Would it help if I told you that I can narrow it down to one of two candidates?'

Kelly tried hard not to think about how such an item might get dislodged in the vicinity of Jason's desk and just what kind of helping hand he'd had in the matter. 'Nope. But that's because it's none of my business what you get up to once I've gone home for the evening. You could have a whole… *herd*…of girls up here for all I care.'

The mischievous grin remained, but his eyes searched her features as if he was trying to work out if she was telling the truth. She made sure she gave him no clues.

'And while we're on the subject, Amber called again.'

There it was, the shifty expression she'd been waiting for…. Jason didn't have to open his mouth to let her know that poor Amber was history.

'Don't you give me that look…that boyish, won't-you-take-pity-on-me look! I've told you already that you can tidy up your own messes. You've made your bed, as my grandmother used to say, and now you've got to lie in it. Just tell the poor woman it's over!'

'I have,' Jason muttered, 'and it's not the bed bit that's the problem.'

Kelly pretended she hadn't heard. She sighed and shook her head. 'Honestly, what do you do to these women to make them so…so…whatever they are?'

He opened his mouth, but Kelly held up a hand. 'Scratch that. I don't want to know how—' She clamped her mouth shut before she could dig herself in any deeper.

The smile playing round the edges of his eyes was pure devilment. 'How *what*?'

She licked her lips. She had been going to say *how good in bed you are,* but had managed to put the brakes on at the last second. Seemed that working for Jason was teaching her new skills in self-control.

'How you...hypnotise...them,' she finally said, watching Jason's smile grow slowly even more wicked. 'At least, that's what I assume you do, because any woman in possession of her full senses would see through you in a flash.'

'Like you do,' he said, his voice low and velvety.

'Precisely.' She straightened her spine, turned and walked away, ignoring the knowledge that he was silently laughing at her as she headed back to the safety of her desk.

But at least he hadn't pressed the matter or decided he was in a teasing kind of mood. She really *didn't* want to know how good in bed he was. Chloe would say it was because she'd regret what she was missing, but it wasn't that. When the sex was good, it was a nice extra in a relationship, but it couldn't be the foundation. She'd had that kind of chemistry with Tim and look how well that had turned out.

Oh, she knew it wasn't always a disaster—Chloe and Dan being a case in point—but good sex, even off-the-charts sex wasn't a guarantee of any sort, even if those wonderful endorphins it produced were such good liars, telling you it meant something when it didn't, making you feel that something cosmically earth-shattering had occurred, when really it was just some well-designed biology to keep the species going.

She didn't believe in 'soulmates' anymore. You just had to find a good match, someone you got on with, who wanted the same things out of life as you did, and if there was a spark there so much the better.

Never again would she be one of those silly women like the ones on Jason's list. The ones who believed too much, who saw a god when there was really only an ordinary fallible man. No, Kelly had her eyes open now, and she was never going to be tricked that way again. The happiness of her and her boys depended on it.

CHAPTER SIX

KELLY ARRIVED AT Greenwich Park the following Saturday with a firm grip on each of her sons and a cool bag slung across her body. The strap dug into her shoulder more with every step, but she wasn't going to let go of Cal and Ben until they'd reached their destination. There was no telling where they'd run off to otherwise and the park was a big place.

Thankfully, she soon found some faces she recognised on a flat expanse of grass just before the landscape dipped dramatically to meet the Thames. Across the river, the sun glinted off the skyscrapers in Canary Wharf. It seemed odd for the towering buildings to be so close when she was standing in a royal park that was so old the sense of a rural idyll still clung about it.

She sighed and looked up at the bright sun climbing steadily in the sky. Weather forecasting was obviously not her talent, because the day was as clear and warm as any that blessed Los Angeles.

Well, that was what Kelly imagined. The furthest west she'd ever been was St Ives.

As they neared the growing sprawl of Aspire employees, she tried to stop herself scanning the crowd for Jason. And failed miserably.

It didn't matter. He wasn't there yet. She shook her head and concentrated on laying a tartan blanket out on the warm grass, forbidding herself from looking up and checking for who else had arrived once she'd finished. That done, she sat down and leaned back on her hands, legs stretched in front of her, enjoying the sun on her face and the slight breeze that ruffled the loose hair around her shoulders.

At least, she enjoyed it until she was felled by two small boys who'd launched themselves at her. They were alternately strangling her, bouncing up and down and eyeing the play park at the bottom of the vast hill.

'Can we go to the swings, Mummy? Can we? Can we? *Please?*'

Kelly unhooked Ben's arm from around her windpipe and gasped for some oxygen before she answered. 'Maybe after lunch,' she told them, then pointed over to a blanket not far away, where Sarah from Accounting, her husband and brood of four children were gathered. 'There are some kids your age over there. Why don't you see if you can go and play with them?'

Cal pulled a face. 'They're *girls*.'

She smothered a smile. 'Well, those *girls* have got a football in their bag. Still not interested in playing with them?'

The boys exchanged looks. Cal looked down and scuffed the grass with his trainer, before staring longingly at the assortment of brightly coloured pint-sized sports equipment being unloaded from a large holdall.

'I suppose we could go and teach them how to play properly,' he said slowly.

Once again, Kelly struggled to keep her lips in a straight line. From the look of the pink-and-lilac-clad tomboys clambering over their father to get to the toys, they could teach Ben and Cal a thing or two.

She pushed herself to her feet. 'Come on, we'll go and say hi.'

The boys loped behind her for a few steps, but started running the instant Sarah spotted them coming and beckoned them over. Within thirty seconds Cal was being bossed by Sarah's eldest as to exactly where he should put some discarded cardigans to serve as goalposts. Kelly stood, hands on hips, watching them for a moment and then accepted Sarah's offer to join her on her blanket for a chat.

'So what's the deal with this picnic?' she asked Sarah, keeping half an eye on the game of football that had just started. 'We just slowly toast ourselves in the sunshine and stuff our faces?'

Sarah grinned at her as she rolled up her T-shirt sleeves to expose her shoulders. 'If that's what you want, but this being a sporty kind of staff, there's also a chance to burn off the picnic calories, should you wish to. Jason's big on organising games and races and getting the different departments to compete against each other.'

Kelly stared ahead and said nothing. Of course he was.

'Highlight of the afternoon is the annual rounders tournament. Of course, Jason calls it baseball, and we don't correct him, but we all know it's really good old British rounders. Production and Design won last year and they're determined to hold on to their trophy.'

Kelly closed her eyes. 'Please don't tell me there's an actual trophy.'

Sarah chuckled. 'Of course there's a trophy! It's all the guys talk about. It gives them gloating rights for the next twelve months.' Her mouth hitched up at one side. 'The way they go on about it, you'd think the stupid thing had magical powers. You watch, they'll be warming up and taking their practice swings before lunch.'

Sarah was right about that. Not ten minutes passed before a band of serious-looking twenty-somethings, all with specially printed T-shirts with the Aspire logo and 'P & D' on the back, huddled together and started taking turns with a bat. Kelly only half watched them, content to just sit and do nothing for once. Sarah's husband was supervising the kiddie football game, so she didn't even have to keep more than half an ear out for her sons' voices.

For the first time in months, maybe even a couple of years, she felt as if she could kick back and do nothing. It was glorious.

She'd been sitting there quite happily, soaking up the sunshine, when that familiar prickling sensation crept up her arms. She glanced over to where the rounders players were warming up and her stomach lurched so hard she was almost convinced the ground had moved.

There was Jason, in faded jeans and a T-shirt, looking more gorgeous than a man had a right to as he laughed and chatted with some of the other guys. Out of his suit he looked…he looked…

Edible.

Sadly, that was the only word that fitted.

Kelly looked down at her own denim-clad thighs and suddenly wished for her normal temp uniform of skirt and blouse. She hadn't realised they were part of her anti-Jason armour until that moment, but they were. And without her usual uniform the edges of their relationship…well, they seemed too *blurry*.

She discovered she didn't know what to do with herself. The position she was sitting in now seemed posed and fake, but whatever she did with her arms and legs just felt awkward and unnatural. It was as if she was expecting him to look up and notice her sitting there, expecting him to jog over and smile at her before he dropped down on the blanket beside her. And she wasn't. Yes, they worked together, but that didn't mean anything. There were plenty of other people he would want to spend time with today.

However, it was just as well she wasn't secretly hoping Jason would come over and say hi, because for the next half hour he was fully occupied showing young, pretty things—who'd developed a sudden burning passion for rounders—how to hold a bat properly. All of them needed one-to-one tuition, preferably involving Jason wrapping his arms around them from behind and swinging the bat with his large hands covering theirs.

Not that Kelly was paying much attention, although it didn't take more than a quick glance to work out that Jason was loving every second of it.

Still, it irritated her that while she was aware of him maybe fifty feet away, while she could hear the artificially loud giggles of some of his protégées, she just couldn't seem to get back that restful groove she'd had going. Eventually, she stamped to her feet, headed back to her own blanket and started unpacking her and the boys' picnic. They were sure to be hungry soon, what with all that running around Sarah's husband had them doing. And the fending off of yucky girls.

When it was all laid out she called her sons over.

They ran back long enough to grab a packet of crisps each then raced back to their football game. On a normal day, Kelly would have sat them down and made sure they ate a sandwich, but today they were having so much fun she didn't have the heart.

She sighed and picked up a packet herself. The first mouthful confirmed what she'd expected of them. She'd bought them at the pound shop and, while they weren't quite out of date, they had a slight chewiness that suggested they were only just on the right side of staleness.

'Can I have one?'

Kelly stopped chewing for a second and looked up to find Jason towering over her, silhouetted as he blocked out the sun. Unable to talk, she just nodded and watched with big eyes as he dropped gracefully on the blanket beside her and helped himself to a packet of cheese and onion.

'Rounders over for now?' she asked breezily, once she'd swallowed her mouthful of crisp crumbs. 'Only you seemed to have quite a fan club a minute ago.'

Why had she said that? Why? Now he'd know she'd noticed, and she didn't want him knowing that.

Jason just grinned back at her. 'Saving myself for later.'

Stop it, she told her stomach, which did a little flip as his eyes glinted with mischief. *That sort of thing does not appeal to you.*

She sat up and craned her neck. 'Haven't you got an ermine-lined blanket of your own around somewhere?'

Jason just laughed. 'No. I forgot it. But it's nicer to share.'

Kelly looked at the tiny, not-quite-wool tartan rug beneath them. If she'd known that she'd be forced to sit quite this close to him, she might have invested in one that was…oh…twenty times larger?

'Well, the crisps are all you're having off me. I didn't bring a lot.' She looked down at the little cling-film-wrapped packets of sandwiches and assortment of fruit in the centre of the rug. There were three chocolate biscuits also lurking in the bottom of the cool bag, but Kelly wasn't giving hers up for anybody.

He reached behind him and pulled a proper wicker picnic basket with leather buckles forward. 'I said I'd forgotten the blanket, not the food.' His

gaze flitted to her meagre provisions. 'You're shar-
ing your blanket. Care to share my lunch?'

Something inside Kelly nosedived. Ah. That was
it. He was taking pity on her. That was why he was
here, clogging up her blanket when he could have
been lolling around somewhere else with a leggy
blonde wrapped around him.

She was about to open her mouth and tell him exactly where he could shove his fancy picnic, sandwich by sandwich, when he added, 'My mother
has this monstrosity sent to me from Fortnum's
every year, just for the company picnic. I think
she thinks that because I'm in London the Queen
might just wander past and I'd better be properly
provisioned, just in case.'

Now he'd made her laugh, which had so *not* been
part of the plan. And when he opened the hamper
up, she could see all sorts of delicious things in
there…proper ham, not the watery packet stuff,
pâté, scones, clotted cream. Her stomach growled
and she decided that maybe she could take pity on
her boss and help him out. Just this once.

He offered her a savoury minimuffin and she
took it without hesitation. It was soft and slightly

cheesy, with a hint of basil and sun-dried tomatoes. Heaven.

At that moment the boys rushed up. It seemed Sarah's husband was in the mood for food too and had broken up the game to investigate his own picnic hamper. Both Cal and Ben skidded to a halt at the edge of the picnic blanket and stared at Jason.

'Who are you?' Ben said, with no hint of wariness in his tone, just curiosity.

Jason held up a hand for a high five, which Ben jumped for and slapped. 'I'm Jason. I work with your mom,' he said and held his hand out for his older brother. Cal shook his head and sidled towards Kelly a bit.

'Your voice sounds funny,' Ben said. 'Are you from the telly? I've heard people talk like you on the telly.'

Jason grinned at the little boy. 'Nope. Not from the TV. Just America. And, to me, you're the ones with the funny voices.'

Ben just giggled. 'My voice isn't funny, but Mummy's sometimes is. Especially when she's cross and she's—'

'Ben, why don't you stop pestering Jason and sit down and eat your sandwiches?'

Her youngest gave Jason a look that said, *See?*

Jason leaned in and spoke in a stage whisper behind his hand. 'She uses that voice on me too.'

Cal couldn't help joining in after that. 'Are you naughty too sometimes?' he asked as he sat down right next to Kelly, half on one of her feet.

Jason winked. 'Sometimes.'

'Always,' Kelly said, and all three males shared a conspiratorial chuckle.

Great. Three seconds in his company and her kids had turned traitor and teamed up with Jason. This afternoon was going to be just peachy. She should have known, though. Of course Jason would get on with her kids…being such a big kid himself.

She unwrapped Ben's sandwich and handed it to him. He handed it back to her.

'What?' she said. 'It's ham. You like ham.'

'It's pink,' Ben replied, crossing his arms. 'Only girls eat pink stuff.'

Kelly raised an eyebrow. 'Really? You didn't seem to mind much last week when you were scoffing your way through Auntie Chloe's cupcakes.'

'I want to eat meat.'

Kelly shook her head slightly. 'Ham *is* meat.'

Ben gave her a superior kind of look. 'I want red meat.'

'Red meat…?' What on earth was he talking about? Most meat was brown, maybe off-white. What the heck was Tim feeding them when they went to stay with him?

Ben nodded. 'Like dinosaurs. I want to be a dinosaur. T-rex eats his meat all red and drippy.'

Her child wanted to eat raw meat. O-kay.

'Look, Ben, you're just going to have to take my word for it. Ham is meat and it's not girly.'

Ben's brows bunched together. 'Won't.'

'Hey, buddy…' Ben swung his head round to look at Jason. 'Do I look girly to you?' And he made a fist and displayed his rather fine biceps to make his point. Kelly's mouth went dry.

Ben shook his head.

'Then pass me one of those sandwiches, will you?'

Ben, keen to join in the game, leapt up and handed Jason one of his sandwich triangles. Jason made a big show of eating it all up and rubbing his stomach afterwards. 'Yummy.'

Ben's eyes were wide, but he didn't make a move towards his lunch. Kelly knew just how stubborn her youngest could be. If Ben had decided the sky was luminous purple, then luminous purple it would stay—until he woke up one morning and decided it was zebra striped instead.

Jason's eyes narrowed slightly as he studied the little boy sitting across the picnic blanket from him. He leaned forward and lowered his voice. 'As well as being your mom's boss, the other thing you don't know about me is that I'm half dinosaur.' He said it so seriously that Cal, who'd begun to giggle, went quiet. Jason looked between the two boys and then he let out a low, rasping noise, similar to the ones the dinosaurs made in Ben's favourite animated film. Before Kelly could react, he jumped to his feet, elbows clamped to his side, and started doing a pretty passable impression of a T-rex.

Kelly pressed her fingers over her lips and tried to suppress a laugh as her boys squealed and ran away across the grass. Jason lumbered after them, still in character, and chased them round for a couple of minutes before picking them up, tucking one under each arm and stomping back to the picnic blanket with them. Most of the Aspire team had stopped eating their picnics to watch the goings-on, and when Jason deposited first one boy then the other—head first—onto Kelly's blanket, they cheered and gave him a round of applause.

Jason took a bow then dropped back down on the ground, looking one hundred per cent human again. He turned to Ben. 'So…if I can eat a ham sandwich, I'm sure you can.'

'I can't believe you just did that,' Kelly whispered, not completely able to keep the smile from her lips. 'Everyone was watching.'

Jason just shrugged. *So?* his shoulders said. He didn't care.

Of course he didn't care. Jason didn't care about anything. Except his Mercury running shoes.

'Worked, didn't it?' he said as Ben tucked into his sandwich, making baby dinosaur noises between mouthfuls.

Kelly sighed. 'There's no hope, is there? Raw meat? He's a proper man already. Next thing we know, he'll be firing up a barbecue and asking for a beer.' Then she smiled at Jason, a soft, thankful smile, for once completely unlaced with sarcasm.

He grinned back at her. 'You're welcome.' And, instead of the devilish glint she'd come to expect, the look in his eyes was warm and honest and… Jason.

For the longest moment they stayed like that, and

then Kelly looked away, fussed with the cool bag and then resorted to unwrapping the sandwich she no longer had an appetite for. He had no business being all *Jason* with her. She'd rather he was that guy who'd been helping the bimbos to bat. That guy was much easier to resist.

'You are going to help me eat this, aren't you?' he asked her. 'I can't believe that tiny little sandwich is going to fill you up.' And he waved a real plate under her nose, on which sat a piece of perfectly pink salmon fillet and a dollop of creamy-looking coleslaw. Kelly was a sucker for coleslaw.

She let out a theatrical sigh. 'If I *have* to...but just remember, if I do this for you, you'll owe me.'

'Of course,' he replied, and she could hear the mirth in his tone, but she dared not look him in the eye. It would be too easy, too easy to feel as if this was normal, as if he should always fill the empty spot on her picnic blanket, but they both knew he wasn't auditioning for that job.

But it didn't help when, after lunch, he urged the boys to join in the kids' rounders game, then volunteered to teach them how to swing a bat when they said they didn't know how.

They should know, Kelly thought. That was

something Tim should have taught them, not a stranger barely an hour after their first meeting.

She should have known something was inherently wrong with Tim right from the start. He'd never seemed quite as into spending time with his sons as her friends' husbands had been. Oh, he'd done it. Sometimes. But there'd always been a look hidden behind his smile that suggested he couldn't quite get the minutes to tick away fast enough so he could do something he wanted instead.

She'd thought Tim and Jason had been like peas in a pod when she'd first met her boss but, watching him disappoint the pouting girls who were hoping for a refresher course before the big game so he could patiently show a four-year-old how to hold a rounders bat, she realised she couldn't have been more wrong. On the surface, maybe, but deep underneath, where it mattered, there was something *more* to Jason, something that had been missing in her ex-husband. Which led to a scary kind of logic: If having that piece missing meant there had been something inherently wrong with Tim, did that mean there was something inherently *right* with Jason?

When he finally tired the boys out and they begged to come and have more food, all three rejoined her on the blanket. She reached over and ruffled Ben's hair as he dived head first into the cool bag in search of his chocolate biscuit.

'You're good with them,' she told Jason, looking longingly at her smallest son, feeling her heart warm at the sight of his mouth smeared with chocolate after just one bite. 'I suppose that comes from being a big brother.' She raised her eyes to meet Jason's. 'Is there much of an age difference?'

His smile froze, just for a split second. 'Four years.'

'You must have felt very protective towards him.'

Jason shrugged. 'Guess so.' He nodded towards the boys. 'But you know what brothers are like. We fought more than we bonded.' And then he stared out across the park to the glinting skyscrapers on the other side of the river.

'You don't talk about your family much.'

Jason continued to stare at the skyline. 'Not much to say. I'm the black sheep, so nobody minds if communication is patchy. Frankly, I think my father prefers it that way.'

'What about your mother? You keep in contact with her, right?'

He shrugged. 'I don't know what my mother was like when she was younger, but now she's more like my father's shadow than his wife. And if he thinks I need to be left out in the cold for a while so I can see the error of my ways…well, my mother wouldn't dare disagree.'

Kelly leaned in closer and spoke softly. 'But she sends you the hamper every year—the best money can buy. I bet she sends you other things too, little things she knows you'd like.'

Jason turned and looked at her, surprise and dawning realisation on his features.

'Perhaps you should give her a call once in a while,' Kelly said, looking away and staring at the view Jason had found so riveting. 'Mothers know they have to let their sons go one day. Doesn't mean it doesn't hurt to do it…or even think about it.'

She could feel Jason looking at her and ignored it for as long as she could, but eventually she caved and turned her head.

'I'm seeing a whole new side to you today, Kelly.'

Ditto. But she wasn't going to tell him that.

Instead she gave him one of her patented haughty looks. 'Don't get used to it,' she told him. 'Come Monday morning, it'll be business as usual.'

CHAPTER SEVEN

THERE WAS NOTHING Jason liked better than a competitive game, even if it was only with a stumpy version of a baseball bat and a tennis ball, and the company rounders tournament was no exception. Each year he joined a different team rather than just creating a senior management team that everyone was afraid to win against. Where would be the fun in that? For a competition to be exciting it had to have a real threat of defeat, otherwise the adrenalin zing that victory always brought would be missing.

This year he'd joined the Secretaries and Stuff team. Self-named and totally intent on putting their bosses in their places, even if their battle readiness outstripped their ability. And it hadn't been because Kelly was on the team. Because she hadn't been. Not until they'd realised they were one short because of a no-show and he'd convinced her to join them.

'I'll show you how to hold the bat, if you like,' he'd told her.

She'd just scrunched up her face and shook her head. 'First, I've seen what your version of *showing* entails, thank you very much. Besides, I have two burly older brothers. Do you really think I don't know how to play rounders?'

'And second?'

She smiled sweetly at him. 'You, in particular, don't want to be within hitting distance when I have one of these in my hands.' And then she'd marched off to take her place in the line, ready to take her turn. Jason had just laughed as he'd watched her go.

Pity.

He'd have liked a seemingly innocent excuse to get closer to Kelly, more than just a handshake. While he'd totally enjoyed his tuition session with some of the female staff earlier on—even if he'd been able to sense Julie's disapproving glare from under the large chestnut tree on the fringes of the picnic area—he hadn't been able to help wishing it wasn't a fresh, young twenty-something pressing herself against his front as he put his arms around her and guided her hands into the right grip on the bat. He realised he'd wished it was a certain single mom instead.

The need to smell that perfume of hers again had blindsided him. He didn't just want to get a waft as she walked by him in the office, but up close and on her skin, the way perfume was meant to be smelt.

And he couldn't quite get that idea out of his head as the game progressed.

It was weird, because he hadn't thought seeing her with her boys would have been so appealing. He didn't mind the single-mom thing, had dated plenty of them, but this was the first time it had made him want a woman more.

Kelly was different with her kids around. He'd seen a softer side to her, one that she usually hid. And she was amazing with Ben and Cal. They'd got frustrated at not being able to hit the ball at first but, instead of losing patience with them—as his own father had—and telling them to stop whining and just suck it up, she'd encouraged them. She'd reminded them it was only their first time and just how hard they'd found it to kick a football far when they'd first started. He also liked that she hadn't given them false praise. She'd agreed they weren't superstars but she also hadn't pretended their frustration didn't matter.

She loved them the same way she did everything else, he realised, with openness and honesty, and that was a rare thing. He'd thought her guarded and prickly, but maybe she needed to be because it was obvious to anyone with eyes that when Kelly gave herself, she gave herself completely. Those boys were lucky. They were going to grow up feeling secure with their place in the world because of the gift she gave them every day. So many kids weren't that blessed.

There were cheers when she took her turn to bat. She'd only been at Aspire a few months, but she was already a popular member of staff. He'd have to talk to Julie about her future with the company. They'd be all the poorer if they lost her to someone else after the temp contract came to an end.

The bowler narrowed his eyes and focused on the slim, long-limbed woman brandishing the bat. He swung and released the ball. A split second later it cracked against the wood and shot off to the right, sending the fielders running. Kelly threw the bat behind her and sprinted off round the pitch. Their team went wild, yelling and whooping and cheering her on. Jason joined them, and when she shot past fourth base and into the arms of a squealing bunch of women, he had to concentrate on rooting himself to the spot so he didn't plough through them, peel them off her and do the same.

Something began to buzz in the pit of his stomach. Something warm and tingly that he hadn't experienced before. It worried him slightly. Enough to stop him following through on his urge, anyway.

She joined the end of the line, right behind him. He held up a palm for a high five and she grimaced before smacking it.

'You hit that ball like you meant it,' he told her.

'I did,' she said, grinning just a little too widely for comfort. A nasty thought sneaked up on him.

'It wasn't my head you were visualising hitting, was it?'

She laughed. 'No... That honour was reserved for my ex,' she admitted, then frowned as she scanned the crowd.

'Problem?' he asked her.

She shook her head. 'No, just looking for someone. Inspiration for hit number two.'

Jason stopped grinning. 'He's not here.'

She stopped searching the crowd and searched his face instead. 'Who?'

'Payne.'

Her mouth dropped open, just a little.

'I fired him a couple of weeks ago,' he said.

She pressed a palm to her chest. 'Because of me?'

He shrugged. 'Because of a lot of things but, yes, your complaint was part of it.' And then, because she was looking at him all wide-eyed and soft, because he was worried he liked her looking at him as if he was some knight in shining armour, he forced himself to shrug it off. 'Darn your civilised employment laws. If I'd had my way, I'd have creamed the guy months ago, not jumped through hoop after hoop to get rid of him.'

But the implication of violence on his part didn't seem to put her off any. If anything, she was softening further under his gaze.

'Thank you,' she whispered.

He looked away. 'No problem. I did it for Aspire. We don't need jerks like him on our team.'

Liar, a little voice inside his head whispered. You know why you really did it. And you know why you really wanted to beat the loser into a pulp.

Jason ignored the voice. Instead he turned and focused on the rest of the game, cheering the other players on and feeling slightly relieved when he and Kelly ended up at far ends of the grassy expanse when it was time to field. This wasn't the time to change his game plan and get serious about a woman. And this was not the woman to get serious with. She didn't want a guy like him in her life. Strangely, he couldn't help but think she was right.

When the game finished, Secretaries and Stuff coming in a respectable third, they made their way back to Kelly's picnic blanket. He had to, so he could collect his mother's idea of an informal lunch.

Kelly called the boys over, who'd been losing a wrestling bout with Sarah's three daughters, and she started to pack her things away.

'Are you going home?'

She nodded. 'Not only are the boys worn out, but it's a long trip home. I know this isn't far from the offices, but I have quite a long commute.'

As if on cue, Cal yawned. Kelly smiled at him, then bent to kiss the top of his head. 'If we don't set off now we'll be really late home for tea, and you don't want to know just how grouchy my little dinosaurs get when they're hungry.'

Ben looked up at her. 'Mum? Can't Jason come home with us for tea?'

Kelly stopped what she was doing and stood up. It was a couple of moments before she met Jason's eyes. 'Would you? Like to come back for something to eat? It's the least I could do after the help you've been this afternoon.'

Normally Jason would have sprinted away as fast as the famous Dale McGrath at such an invitation, but he discovered he wanted to say yes. 'I could drive,' he found himself saying, 'save you the Tube journey.'

She just looked at him. Not the normal, half-suspicious surveillance, but an open and unguarded look, as if she was trying to see inside his head and read what was there. And he let her. He let her see because, for once in his life, he couldn't be bothered to find an angle to play. Whatever she saw, it surprised her, because her eyes widened just a fraction, but she still didn't look away.

The sounds of the park faded. All Jason was aware of was a pair of big grey-green eyes staring back at him, the dark lashes framing them, the rise and fall of her ribcage in time with his own.

Suddenly he understood that what they were considering would mean crossing a line. Not just between professional and private, office and home, but something deeper, something less easily defined and much more dangerous.

It was Kelly who broke away first. She looked away across the park, then back at him. 'Tell me one thing, Jason.'

He swallowed. The mood had gotten very serious and he had a feeling that whatever she was about to ask was very important.

His throat felt tight when he answered. 'Sure. Fire away.'

'Do you own a set of golf clubs?'

He blinked. *That* was the all-important question? He almost laughed it off, but she was looking at him intently, waiting for his answer.

'Uh-huh.'

She considered that for a moment. 'And where do you keep them?'

He frowned and opened up his mouth to ask where the heck this line of interrogation was going but she held up a hand.

'Just humour me, will you?'

Jason shrugged. It wasn't top-secret information. 'At the moment, they're gathering dust in my hall closet,' he told her and paused for a moment, calculating just how long they'd been there. 'I really should get back to golf some time soon….'

Kelly nodded, more to herself than to him, and hitched the cool bag higher on her shoulder. 'Actually, I'm exhausted too. I'll probably just resort to beans on toast when we get in…' She shrugged. 'But maybe another time?'

He nodded because he was supposed to. 'Sure.'

She held out a hand for each boy. 'Come on, you two.'

They paused as their gazes snagged again and silent communication zapped between them. He nodded. 'See you Monday.'

She tried a smile that didn't quite fit. 'Monday,' she repeated, and then she turned and walked away without looking back.

Jason let out a sigh then looked at the sky. He'd always said she was a smart lady, and she'd just proved him right again, had saved them both from something that would only have gotten messy and complicated. He understood. Hell, he even agreed.

But that didn't mean he didn't stop thinking about her as he offloaded the rest of his mother's fancy picnic on his employees. And that didn't mean that when he set off for his car, empty hamper swinging from his hand, he didn't think of his riverside apartment and how large and empty it would feel when he stepped inside it that evening.

Kelly walked into Jason's office on Monday morning with her blouse and skirt pressed to perfection and her chin lifted high. Back to normal. Fantastic.

But as she got closer to the desk she realised that, even though Jason was wearing a suit, she could still see the man with the soft blue jeans and sun lighting up his dark hair. She could still see the man who'd pretended to be a dinosaur so a little boy would eat his lunch.

The word that echoed round her head was not one she'd have wanted her kids repeating.

She stretched her smile wide as he looked up. He seemed slightly taken aback, as if her unusually bright grin was blinding him a little, but he smiled back. A half sort of smile, not a full-on Jason sort of smile.

'What's up?' she asked.

He pressed his lips together and shook his head. 'Nothing. In fact, everything is going great. I have the contract for the endorsement deal in front of me. One signature and Miles Benson, supreme decathlon champion, is ours.'

He stared at the bit of paper and his pen stayed where it was on the desk, lying perfectly perpendicular to the top of the contract.

'So why don't you sign it?'

Jason looked up at her, a slight frown crinkling his forehead. 'I will. I just... It feels like it should be a *moment*, and this doesn't feel like a moment.' His eyebrows shot up. 'Don't you think it should be...?'

She gave him a wry look. 'A moment?'

Jason shook his head and looked away. Kelly studied him. For a man who sometimes had more bounce than an excited Labrador, he was awfully still and quiet this morning.

She walked over to the bookcase and picked up the picture of Jason with his father and brother. She'd seen the photo a hundred times, but suddenly she sensed something in the body language, in just the *feel* of the image that she hadn't noticed before. After placing it back on the shelf, she turned to

Jason. 'He's the favourite, isn't he?' she said, nodding back at the picture.

Jason didn't look at it. 'Yes.' He sighed. 'But he deserves to be.'

'No parent should pick and choose. I love both my boys the same, even if they're very different.'

Jason shrugged. 'Families like mine can't help themselves. It's all about being the best, having the most. They can't just switch it off when the kids come along.'

She shook her head. A family didn't have to be rich and powerful to have favourites. Just look at her father! He'd adored his two strapping lads, but hadn't known quite what to do when a little girl had unexpectedly joined their family. She'd had to be twice as much of a boy as Dan and Jonathan to keep up, and even then there had never quite been the same glow of pride in their father's eye for her as there had been for her brothers.

'But that doesn't mean you have to accept it,' she told him. 'That doesn't mean it's right. You have to fight it!'

'No point,' Jason said, shaking his head. 'It doesn't matter what I do now. Brad's already won. He's triumphed through the adversity I caused.

He's got the gold medal that I'll never have. No one can compete with that.'

'But you still try,' she said quietly, because that was what the shoes were about really. Suddenly it all made sense.

Jason huffed and stood up to look out of the window across the London skyline. 'For all the good it does.'

'Don't you dare give up!' She shocked herself at the vehemence of her outburst. 'Those shoes are good and you know they are.'

Jason turned round and leaned against the window. 'I know that.'

She walked over to stand next to him, nodded over her shoulder at the paperwork on his desk. 'So sign…'

Jason just heaved in a breath and let it out again.

'You don't want to.'

He turned and looked at her, the truth as evident in his eyes as the crumbs on Cal's shirt after he'd raided the biscuit tin.

'As good as Benson is, you don't want him, do you? You still want McGrath.'

He exhaled heavily. 'I can't envision the whole

thing without him. He's the best. And with him on board, people would have to take notice.'

Jason might have said *people*, but Kelly heard the silent word behind it. My *father* would have to take notice....

She recognised this for what it was: defeat mixed in with an unhealthy dollop of self-pity. Kelly didn't like self-pity. It sucked the life out of a person. She should know. She'd almost succumbed to it when the cancer diagnosis had come and Tim had left. But then she'd got angry. Fighting angry. And that fight had got her through.

She took a deep breath. By saying what she was going to say next she might just find a boot in her backside and security officers to escort her to the front door, but she was going to be doing Jason a favour. He needed the same kind of medicine she'd had, and she was going to make him take it.

She put her hands on her hips and stared him down. 'You're a coward,' she said. 'You're too scared to go after what you really want, and you're letting Mercury down by settling for second best. And if your heart's not in it, Mercury will flop and you'll prove to them—to everyone, including your father—that you *aren't* up to it.'

His eyes narrowed as he looked back at her and—*whoomph!*—it was like a pilot light had ignited a boiler behind them. Kelly fought back a smile.

'I didn't give up and I didn't settle for second best,' he said with a clenched jaw. 'I put everything into that promotional package, but McGrath wouldn't listen.' His voice rose in volume as he reached the end of his speech and Kelly knew her plan was working.

'Then tear up this contract and go after what you want. Care enough to take a risk rather than going for the easy option!' she yelled back at him. '*Make McGrath listen!*'

Jason just stared at her, looking as if he'd like to set her alight.

'I researched him,' she said, 'after he knocked us back.'

Jason shook his head. 'You don't think I did that before I jumped into this? I know everything about the man—what his kids are called, what subjects he studied at school, even his dog's name! None of it helped.'

Kelly walked back to Jason's desk and rested her backside on the edge of it, folding her arms.

'The presentation was cool, it was fun, it was everything you wanted it to be but, at the end of the day, it was all smoke and mirrors, and that's not what McGrath responds to.'

He gave her a disbelieving look.

'Think about it! You know what a lot of sprinters are like—they swagger, pose for the cameras, show how cool they are before a race. Does McGrath do any of that?'

Jason blinked, and then after a few seconds he shook his head. 'I thought the video rocked,' he said, just a little defensively.

'It did!' Kelly replied, excitement making her pitch rise. 'But I think you need to save all that slickness for the ad campaign. McGrath is a cool customer. He's *serious* about running. He doesn't even pretend it's no big deal like the rest of them do. I think he wants a *serious* shoe—and that's not what we showed him.'

Jason frowned. 'Keep talking.'

'You and I know that Mercury *is* a serious shoe. Maybe we don't need all that glitz and hype. That's what people do to dress something up when it's not very good. And I know that you believe in this product. I see it in the way you talk about it, how dedicated you are to it. You made *me* believe in Mercury and I think you can do the same for Dale McGrath.'

The fire in Jason's eyes solidified into determination. 'Okay, I'm biting. But isn't this shutting the stable door after the horse has bolted?'

Kelly smiled. 'You're a pretty persistent kind of guy, you know. I reckon if you transferred some of that energy into courting McGrath instead of chasing the female population of London around, you'd have a pretty good chance. What you need to do is get McGrath to talk to you face to face—solo—without all the glossy brochures and the spinning logos. I reckon you'd have him sold in under an hour.'

Jason's stern expression melted. 'Thank you,' he said, looking straight into her eyes, 'for giving it to me straight.'

Kelly felt her cheeks heat and she looked away. 'Just trying to protect my own backside,' she mumbled. 'I need this job.'

He walked back over to his desk, dropped into his chair and fired up his laptop. 'He's not due back in London for months.'

Kelly shook her head. Men! They were always so literal.

'Then don't see him in London,' she said softly. 'Go to New York and see him there.'

He froze. She knew the idea had just slammed into his brain and he was taking time to process it. And when she saw him nod, she could tell he knew it made sense.

'Okay...I will,' he said, and then he looked up at her. Right into her, it seemed. 'But on one condition.'

One corner of Jason's mouth hitched and she got caught up in looking at it. 'And what's that?' she asked, her voice shaky. For some reason she was having a severe and extremely lucid flashback of that kiss outside the Tube station, remembering how good that mouth had felt against her lips.

'You come with me,' he said.

CHAPTER EIGHT

'GO, FOR GOODNESS' sake!' Chloe said and pushed Ben high on the swing.

Kelly squinted at her in the low sun. There'd been just enough time to get a trip to the park in before bedtime. She sighed. Thank goodness for long summer evenings. Sometimes, despite all the mayhem her boys caused, she longed for those days when she'd been a stay-at-home mum and hadn't had to snatch time with them at odd hours of the day. The rest of the park was practically deserted, most of the other kids having visited after school before they went home for dinner.

'I can't just drop everything and flit off for four days!' she said, keeping an eye on Cal, who she was trying to teach to swing under his own steam. 'It's impossible.'

Her son was flinging himself backwards and forwards, legs and body working desperately to get up a bit of momentum. Unfortunately, he'd forgotten what Kelly had told him about pushing himself off with his toes and he wasn't going anywhere fast. 'Here, let me get you started,' she told him gently and went to put her hands on his back.

'I want to do it myself!' Cal yelled over his shoulder, frowning, and doubled his frenzied effort.

Kelly rolled her eyes. It didn't matter how beyond him the task was, he never let anyone lend a hand. Why, out of all the qualities she could have passed down to her sons, had it been that dogged stubbornness? Couldn't Tim's anything-for-an-easy-life genes have cancelled things out a bit? He hadn't been able to stick at anything for too long. Especially marriage.

She caught her sister-in-law's eye and found her smiling. Kelly knew exactly what was going through her brain.

'Stop it,' she said.

She was *not* being stubborn about going to New York with Jason. She was being practical.

'But you've always wanted to go,' Chloe said, a little too reasonably for Kelly's tastes. 'The Empire State Building…Central Park…Little Italy…. Now's your chance! And you'd get to go business class, stay in a nice hotel—it *will* be a nice hotel, won't it?'

Kelly nodded reluctantly. 'I expect so. Jason does seem to like the finer things in life.'

Chloe leaned over and gave her a nudge. 'He likes *you...*'

'Stop it,' Kelly said again. 'I used to think you were fairly sane until you married my brother, but he's having a bad influence on you. Now you're just as pushy as the rest of the Bradfords.'

Chloe smiled sweetly at her. 'I like to think of it as having discovered my inner mule.'

Kelly snorted. She didn't like it much, whatever it was. 'It was supposed to be the other way around,' she said mournfully. 'You were supposed to mellow him out a bit.'

'I just want to see you have a little fun, Kells. You deserve it.'

There was that. But there was fun and there was *fun*. Chloe's version was all tied up with a pair of long legs, some broad shoulders and a devilish grin. 'I married that particular brand of fun and ended up in the divorce court,' she told Chloe, 'which turned out not to be so hilarious after all.

I think I've had enough of feckless men to last me a lifetime.'

Chloe made a scoffing noise. 'I'm not suggesting you marry this one,' she said with a saucy glint in her eye, 'just that you have a little—'

'Fun?' Kelly interjected, her voice low and grim.

Chloe shrugged. 'I was going to say *fling*, but whatever.'

Cal had obviously worn himself out with his flapping backwards and forwards and decided the slide was more appealing. Kelly glanced at the empty seat. Stubborn child.

Ben, as always, copied his brother and dashed off for the slide too. Thankfully, it was the smaller variety, with raised edges and a rubberised floor underneath. She sat down in Cal's empty swing and Chloe came and sat beside her while they both kept a beady eye on the boys a few feet away.

'Okay,' she said slowly, 'say I did decide to go. What would I do with the boys? I can hardly leave them home alone with a can opener and some ready meals.'

Chloe thought for a moment. 'Easy. They can come and stay with us.'

Kelly frowned. 'But I thought your mother was

coming to stay—you've been moaning about it for weeks now.'

'That's what makes it so brilliant,' Chloe said, nodding. 'She can help us with the boys. She'll no doubt *love* showing me just how proper childrearing should be done—'

Kelly muffled a laugh with her hand. 'Good luck with my two!'

Chloe gave her a quick smile then forged on. 'I'll have the perfect excuse not to drag round behind her on her annual shopping spree uptown… and I might even be spared the lecture on having my own offspring before my eggs go bad. Sounds like a win-win deal to me!'

Kelly watched Cal showing Ben how to untangle his legs from underneath himself at the top of the slide and something inside her melted. Stubborn, yes. Generous and caring, also yes. As much as they made her life *interesting* at times, she didn't know what she'd do without her boys.

'Don't you and Dan want kids?' she asked, then realised belatedly it was probably another one of those things she shouldn't bring up.

Chloe sighed.

'Just tell me to shut up,' Kelly said. 'Most people do.'

'It's not that…' Chloe looked at the pale yellow clouds gathering on the horizon. 'I'd love kids, but it's…complicated.' Her expression hardened a little and she turned to Kelly. 'And I'm not doing it just to suit my mother's timetable.'

Kelly nodded. She might be a plain talker, but she could read between the lines as well as the next woman.

So Dan was a little hesitant. It made sense, she supposed. His first marriage had ended catastrophically after his baby son had died, and he and Chloe had only been married a couple of months.

Kelly noticed the sheen in not just her sister-in-law's eyes. 'He'll come around to it,' she told her. 'Just like he did to the idea of marrying again. He just needs a little time to sort it all out in his head.'

Chloe nodded, but her chin crumpled as she said, 'I hope so.'

Kelly was going to put an arm round her, but Chloe pre-empted her by shaking off her pensiveness and smiling brightly at her. She supposed she could help her sister-in-law out by being a distraction technique. Just this once.

'So...' Chloe said, 'now we've got all that sorted out, what shoes are you going to pack for New York?'

Kelly fussed around with her aeroplane seat, putting her laptop in a pocket, stowing away some headphones, rearranging the magazines on offer. She picked up the emergency landing card, grimaced then put it away again. Where could she put her laptop mouse? This was a work trip. She would be working.

'I can't believe they put us in first class,' she muttered for the fifteenth time.

'The benefit of a company frequent-flier account and offices on both sides of the Atlantic,' Jason told her. 'I get upgraded all the time.'

Business class would have been bad enough, thought Kelly. She was used to being in economy with her knees around her chin, but all of this— the comfy seats, three acres of legroom, the proper pillows and polished wood—just made her feel as if she was in a dream, not in the middle of what should be just another working day.

She shouldn't feel this excitement bubbling up in her stomach. Butterflies had arrived that morning before the alarm had gone off, the kind that only usually came with the rumble of case wheels in the pre-dawn quiet or when speeding down a deserted motorway as the sun rose. But this wasn't a holiday; she needed to remember that. So she tried to stamp on the pesky butterflies, but they just flitted up from the floor of her stomach and messed with her heartbeat instead.

She glanced across at Jason, who was looking cool and unconcerned. He was used to this. Even though he'd refused to book first class on the company dollar, she'd bet his family travelled this way all the time. They were certainly rich enough. And if the looming meeting with Dale McGrath was bothering him, he certainly wasn't showing it.

She stared at the blank screen of the personal TV that was presently lying flat against the side of her little cubicle, or whatever they called it. She had to get a grip. This was going to be a long flight and she'd probably be sitting within centimetres of Jason for the whole time, so she really needed to stop *tingling* and just focus on what she was here to do—her job. She slumped back into her comfy seat and sighed. The sooner they took off and she could get her laptop out, the better.

She turned and looked at him. 'We're going to go over the figures again once we're in the air, right? I mean, the one advantage of all this space is that it has to be easier to work, yes?'

'Lots easier to work,' he said, smiling, then prised the laptop mouse she hadn't realised she'd still been clutching out of her hand and tucked it into a convenient side pocket. 'Also lots easier to relax.' He nodded at a rather pretty cabin attendant and she instantly smiled and headed their way with glasses of champagne.

Kelly took the drink but looked at it warily. It wasn't helping with the whole 'remember this is just work' thing. This felt suspiciously like a treat.

'Jeez, Kelly! Unclench a little,' Jason said, laughing slightly, but then his expression became more serious. 'You're not afraid of flying, are you?'

Kelly opened her mouth to say no, she wasn't, but then she closed it again. 'It's been a long time. Not since before I had the boys.... And having kids made me neurotic in all kinds of new and unexpected ways.' Perhaps that was why the butterflies were here. Perhaps that was why she was feeling so out of sorts. Nothing to do with the man sitting next to her at all. 'Maybe I am a little nervous,' she said, almost hopefully.

Jason nudged her champagne glass in her direction. 'Then this will help.'

Kelly sighed and took a sip. It did help. But not in the way she wanted. She wasn't sure she wanted to relax, to get comfortable chatting with Jason as they flew across the ocean. All day.

'So how long has it been since you've been on an aeroplane?' he asked.

She looked at him. Jason wasn't really one for chit-chat. The softness in his eyes confirmed her suspicion—that he was indulging in small talk to make her feel more comfortable, that he was being chivalrous. The rat.

She shrugged. 'Eight years…maybe nine. And I've never done a long-haul flight before. Only quick trips to Spain on package holidays.'

Jason's eyebrows rose higher. 'You've never been to the States before? To New York?'

She shook her head. 'I'd always planned to, though. One day.'

He grinned back at her and the butterflies started doing a clog dance. 'Well, that day is today,' he said, and she couldn't help picking up on some of his infectious enthusiasm. 'We'll have to make sure you see some of the sights.'

Kelly swallowed. She wasn't sure that was a good idea. 'We'll be too busy for that,' she said quickly, hoping that was the case. Jason had been a little tight lipped about the itinerary. 'I'll just grab glimpses as we travel around, maybe do the Empire State Building one evening—if we can squeeze it in.'

But then she thought of standing in the balmy summer-evening air with Jason by her side, staring out across a fairyland of coloured lights and movement, breathing in the energy and magic of the city that never slept, and she started to panic.

Quick. Change the subject. Get it back to something neutral, something less…butterfly encouraging.

'So, will we be dropping in on Knight's head offices while we're there?' she asked him. It seemed like the perfect opportunity. She was curious to find out more about Aspire's parent company.

Jason's grin froze and he knocked back half of his champagne. 'Like you said. Busy schedule. We'll see.'

He didn't say much after that, just stared blankly

at the back of the next row of super-duper lie-flat seats. Kelly breathed out. He'd stopped smiling. He'd stopped looking at her as if something amazing was about to happen and they'd be co-conspirators when it did. That was good. She could breathe again.

But the tingling didn't stop. If anything, it got worse.

Because she could guess what was going on inside his head. Maybe she shouldn't have brought up head office. She knew he had issues with his father, that they ran deep, so why hadn't she just veered away from that subject like a sensible person, kept her nose out and her big mouth shut? *Nice going, Kells.*

She picked up the in-flight magazine and leafed through it as the plane began to taxi towards the runway.

But she knew why she hadn't been able to stay silent. Boys needed their fathers, needed the approval only that central figure in their life could give, and she ached for her two when their dad didn't come to see them as often as he should. Jason might have almost thirty years on her two sons, but the same longing was still there, no matter how hard he clamped it down. And now she was aching for him too, which was way worse than the flickering lust that had waylaid her since the first moment she'd laid eyes on him.

Way worse.

She closed her eyes and let the magazine drop into her lap as the engines began to roar and the plane sped down the runway. She'd been right about one thing: this was going to be a very long flight.

'Wow!'

Jason almost bumped into Kelly and sent her flying. She'd stopped dead in the middle of the hotel lobby and was staring at the ceiling. 'It's a chandelier,' he said. Hadn't she seen one of those before? It wasn't like London didn't have plenty.

Kelly was still staring upwards. 'It's massive.'

'Welcome to the Waldorf Astoria,' he said, grabbing her elbow and trying to get her to move.

Kelly just kept staring at the thousands of glittering crystals above them. 'I can't believe we're staying at the Waldorf,' she said, shaking her head.

Jason groaned inwardly. If they were going to have a repeat of the whole 'first class' thing, he needed a stiff drink. It had taken a couple of hours for that to die.

'It's so beautiful,' she whispered, and then she turned round and noticed the glossy black grand piano sitting on a mezzanine level over the entrance and she let out another gasp of rapture.

Jason watched her with interest. He was quite happy that Kelly had *finally* stopped trying to talk business with him. Who knew all it took was a bit of glittery glass and a marble floor? As much as he appreciated her efforts to support him on this deal—that was why he'd asked her to come, after all—his head was throbbing with all the facts and figures and strategies they'd gone over on the flight. They didn't need them.

But Kelly didn't know that. He hadn't quite told her everything about this trip. Not yet. She was freaked out enough as it was. And she wouldn't understand that this was all part of the game of big business. Going direct to McGrath hadn't helped. This time they needed to plan a little better, manoeuvre. Like chess. Just like chess. But that meant Jason needed to keep a clear head. He needed to still the whirling numbers inside his brain and push them to one side.

What he really needed was a basketball court.

But he was pretty sure the Waldorf didn't have one of those, and they might not appreciate it if he tried to shoot hoops in the grand ballroom. They didn't have a pool either.

But there *was* a Y a couple of blocks away...

He glanced across at Kelly, tugging at her travelling clothes and doing her best not to feel out of place in this rather glitzy New York institution. When he'd booked this hotel he'd thought she'd get a kick out of it, but now he was wondering if the decision hadn't backfired on him a little. She obviously was a little overwhelmed. Which meant she was probably just going to increase her efforts to justify her presence. That meant more facts, more reports to read through. More strategies to discuss...

What he needed to do was distract her. From cluttering up his head again, yes, but also from asking too many questions about when and where they were meeting with McGrath. He'd fibbed a little. Told her they had loose plans for this evening, so it wouldn't be a bad idea to occupy themselves for a couple of hours, doing something that didn't involve talking. Just until he worked it all out in his head.

And the other reason...?

Oh, that.

Well, maybe Kelly herself was a little distracting. Maybe she was adding to this sense of jitteriness he just couldn't shake.

It was weird. Now they were away from the office, things were different. Like they had been the day of the picnic. And he'd spent too long at close quarters with her, inhaling her subtle, slightly spicy perfume, being aware of every move she made, even though their first-class seats had given them ample space. He knew they'd reached a silent understanding to back away from whatever had been building between them, but he was starting to forget why.

Another reason to burn off some of that excess energy fast, before he did something dumb. Again.

So when the receptionist handed him the keys, he handed them straight back to her and asked if their bags could be taken up to their room. Then he grabbed Kelly by the hand and headed down the marble steps to the main entrance.

'Jason! What are you doing?'

'We've had a long journey and we need to do something to unwind before the busy evening ahead.'

She twisted to look over her shoulder and attempted to slip her fingers out of his. 'But the spa's that way…'

He snorted. 'Spas are for wimps,' he told her. 'We're going to do some *real* relaxing! We're going swimming.'

Kelly's mouth worked. 'Swimming? But I don't even have my—'

'Not a problem,' he said as he shoved her into the revolving door and the spinning glass panels cut off the end of her sentence.

As they'd left the Waldorf Jason had pulled out his phone and issued a set of instructions, and by the time they'd arrived at the pool, a mysterious Knight Corporation dogsbody had magically appeared with swimming things for the pair of them in the right size. Kelly didn't want to think about how hard Jason must have been studying her body to get her measurements just right, but at least he'd picked a tasteful one piece instead of a bikini woven from dental floss.

Swimming was the perfect way to clean off the plane dirt, Jason had said, but Kelly wasn't so sure. She'd rather have been doing what her fellow passengers on the flight into JFK were now doing, normal things like zonking out on their ridiculously comfy hotel beds or drinking cocktails.

She slid into the pool, feeling self-conscious and hoping no one was watching, even though the place was virtually deserted. The only other people in the water were a group of guys horsing around and a lone swimmer carving up the water as he did repetitive laps. She should do the same, shouldn't she? She should at least be doing *something* when Jason appeared, and swimming was the obvious choice. Much better than bobbing around in the water chatting with him, trying not to notice both of them had next to nothing on.

God, Kelly. When did you turn into such a prude?

She gave a disgusted half snort, half laugh and launched herself forwards. After she'd swum around for a bit, she glanced back at the changing rooms, expecting to see Jason run from them and soak everyone with a dive-bomb, but there was no sign of him. After a few minutes the group of young guys hauled themselves from the pool and went to dry off. That left her and Mr Serious.

She decided to make the most of the peace and quiet and headed off towards the opposite end of the pool, doing her competent but ungraceful breaststroke. When she reached the tiled edge she hung on gently and breathed out, kicking the water under her feet to stay afloat.

Actually, Jason was right. There was something about the quiet here, the rhythmic splash of the water against the pool's edge and the repetitiveness of the strokes that was soothing. She'd be ready to pass out when they got back to the hotel, though.

She frowned and looked around. Where *was* he? Had he pulled some kind of practical joke on her? She'd be furious with him if he had. But then the serious swimmer drew close once again and, instead of rolling and turning gracefully as he'd done a handful of times since she'd climbed into the pool, he came to a stop and shook the water from his hair.

Kelly wondered if the chlorine in this pool was stronger than she'd been expecting, because her eyes weren't making sense. Mr Serious was trying to morph into Jason. She blinked and rubbed her eyes.

'How are you feeling now?' the blurry blob in front of her asked. 'Better, huh?' And then the pool water cleared from her eyeballs and she was look-ing at her boss.

'Yes,' she said, nodding, hearing the surprise in her own voice. She couldn't quite work out why she hadn't realised the lone swimmer had been Jason, even though it was completely obvious. Must be the jet lag. And maybe the fact that when she'd heard Jason had a failed career as a swimmer, she'd assumed he'd larked around at it for a bit, then got bored and moved on to something else.

But the man in the pool hadn't swum like he'd been larking around. He'd attacked those lengths, eating up the distance with a power that had im-pressed her. And there'd been a grace about him, as if he felt relaxed here. As if this was home.

'Do you miss it?' she asked him. 'Swimming?'

Jason's smile faded and he dragged his hand over his face and hair to wipe away the excess water. 'Yes,' he said simply.

'Why did you stop?'

Nosey, Kelly. You've lectured yourself about this

before, remember? Say the question inside your head before you ask it out loud.

'I injured my shoulder,' he told her. 'It wasn't the same after that.'

'You looked pretty good to me just now.'

See? Now that was another example of her unfiltered comments reaching her mouth. She'd meant it quite innocently, but somehow her voice had grown huskier, and it had added a layer of meaning she hadn't intended. Not consciously, anyway.

Because he did look good. Boy, did he look good.

She was trying hard not to notice, but it was very difficult when those powerful shoulders were only inches away, glistening with pool water. And she couldn't help but take in the tanned skin and the way the chlorine made his eyes go even bluer and his lashes spiky.

'Thanks,' he said, and the lopsided smile he gave her told her he'd registered the gravel in her tone. Despite the cool water lapping around her shoulders, Kelly's cheeks grew hot. In fact, everything grew hot, and all she was aware of was a pair of laughing blue eyes and the silence hanging thick above the water.

She pushed herself away from the side with her feet and floated face up in the water, closing her eyes.

'Don't let me stop you,' she said loudly. 'You carry on doing what you're doing and I'm just going to relax here for a bit.'

And she did just that, floating with her eyes closed, feeling the water lift and fall away underneath her, lulling her into a dreamlike state. Seconds drifted past uncounted until the water swelled beside her and her internal thermostat began to climb again. Jason was near.

'Don't fall asleep,' he said softly.

'I wasn't,' she said, quickly righting herself and treading water.

Jason just gave her one of those twinkly looks. 'Two more minutes and you'd have been gurgling and spluttering and I'd have been pulling you out of the water and giving you the kiss of life.'

Her pulse kicked into high gear at the suggestion. 'In your dreams,' she said and set off swimming towards the changing rooms, not caring if he was ready to leave or not.

And in yours... a little voice whispered as she forced herself not to look back to see if Jason was checking her out as she climbed out of the water.

CHAPTER NINE

KELLY FUSSED WITH the hem of her cocktail dress. She'd been ready to bring just business clothes for the trip, but Chloe had insisted she pack for every eventuality. No suitcase should be without a Little Black Dress, apparently. She'd even lent Kelly a pair of outrageously red stilettos to finish the look off.

Kelly stared at the ornately carved metal doors of the lift and tried not to notice that Chloe's shoes were pinching her little toes. 'What a coincidence that Dale McGrath's hosting a party here at the Waldorf,' she said to Jason.

She was trying not to look at him. Mainly because she hadn't quite recovered from the swimming-pool episode. When he didn't respond to her comment she made the mistake of glancing in his direction, forgetting she'd been trying to keep her eyes on the lift doors. A rush of heat started at her toes and rose up to the tops of her ears.

Even though Jason was looking far too gorgeous to be true in his dark suit and midnight-blue shirt, since the pool she couldn't help picturing him with much less on, little rivulets of pool water running down the muscular contours of his chest. It was most disconcerting.

'Is that why you booked us here?'

'Kinda.' She didn't know how, but she sensed Jason was wearing a grudging smile.

'It was nice of him to invite us.'

'Very.'

'That's a good sign, right? If he's willing to mix with us in a social setting before the official meeting?'

She looked over when he didn't respond immediately. Bad idea. Violent flashback. One involving dark, wet lashes and blue, blue eyes. The breath got stuck somewhere in her chest.

He nodded and the lift doors opened and they stepped inside. He pressed a button for the eighteenth floor and they slid closed again.

Was it hot in here? Kelly was hot.

When they arrived at their floor he guided her into a lobby with a marble floor and a stunning chandelier made of glass feathers. A set of double doors was at the other end, guarded by an attractive blonde with a clipboard. The party was already in full swing. Kelly could see moving lights and milling people and could hear the thump of a popular chart song.

Jason leaned in close and whispered in Kelly's ear, 'You go ahead…. I'll see to this.' And then he walked over to the harried-looking blonde and bestowed his most devastating smile on her. She instantly stopped scowling and smiled back.

Kelly snorted to herself. Now *that* was why she should remember that getting involved with Jason Knight was a bad idea. The man couldn't help himself.

He moved back a few steps as he talked to the blonde and she followed him, stepping away from the door a little. Jason made a shooing motion with his hand, indicating Kelly should go inside without him.

Honestly.

Here she was, all hot and bothered and starting to wonder why she shouldn't just do as Chloe suggested and have a hot New York fling with the man, and he was totally unaffected and chatting up another woman right under her nose!

She huffed to herself then trotted into the party in Chloe's crimson stilettos. The ballroom was long and thin, stretching away from the centre doors to both left and right. Tall French windows with thick damask curtains flanked the space and the gauzy curtains underneath billowed, giving her a glimpse of a short stone terrace. There was a dance floor directly in front of her and at either end of the room, up a couple of steps, were seating areas where guests clustered and chatted or wandered over to the well-stocked bars. All in all, it looked like something out of a Hollywood movie.

Jason appeared by her side, looking a bit too pleased with himself and tucking something into his jacket pocket. A small white business card, if she wasn't mistaken—with numbers scrawled across the back in a looping feminine hand. She raised her eyebrows and gave him a look that said *Really?*

He just grinned back at her. 'I can't help it if she decided she couldn't live without our new line of yoga mats.'

Kelly threw him another one of those looks. This one had shades of *Yeah, right!* attached.

'Let's just find McGrath, do what we've got to

do, say what we've got to say and get out of here.' She frowned and scanned the crowd. 'Now, where is he?'

Moments ago this room had seemed magical, but now the jet lag was sucking away the fairy dust fast, making her feel lethargic and grumpy. At least that was what she ascribed her current mood to. She wasn't prepared to let it be anything else.

Jason didn't join her in her search. In fact, he didn't look particularly enthused at her suggestion. He took the empty glass out of her hand—how had that happened?—and snagged them both another from a passing tray.

'Here,' he said, thrusting it in her direction. 'It's a party. We need to blend in...I mean, chill out. I think we should mingle a bit first.'

She opened her mouth to disagree, but he held up a hand in protest. 'This is a New York moment, right here, and you're missing it! You can't rush this. The Starlight Roof was the place to see and be seen in the thirties and forties. Have you looked up yet?'

Kelly looked up. Above their heads was the most amazing art deco ceiling, covered with a series of stylised metal grilles with central decorations of winged horses and leaping gazelles. 'It's stunning,' she said a little breathlessly.

'We're on the top floor of this section of the hotel. The roof used to retract so the social elite of the day could party underneath the stars.'

So that was where it had got its name. She had wondered.

Kelly had never heard of such a thing. Or been to such a place where people would think it was necessary to roll back the roof to have a good time. It was both wonderful and bemusing. She stopped looking at the ceiling and turned her attention to Jason. He looked completely comfortable with the whole concept. To him, it was just a neat idea. To her, it was a signal of just how different they were, of how she shouldn't get sucked into his world and believe she could be a part of it.

'It's a business trip, Jason. So let's do business.'

'Kelly...' The voice was low and playful. 'Your first time in the Big Apple and you've hardly seen anything more than an anonymous pool and the inside of a hotel suite. Yes, this is business, but the working day ended—' he checked his watch '—*nine* hours ago in London! Why not cut loose and have a little fun? Especially as you've got the chance to mingle with *today's* bright young things…. Look over there!' He pointed to a group huddled on some sofas to their right and Kelly recognised a chart-topping singer and her entourage. 'And there…' A few feet away a group of headline-grabbing sportsmen were arguing about the outcome of a baseball game. 'I can't see McGrath—he may not even have arrived yet. Why not take the chance to have a little fun? When will you ever get the opportunity to do this again?'

Never.

That was the word that rang instantly through Kelly's head.

Jason led her over to a dessert table where there were miniature everythings from pastries to pavlova and layered desserts of different colours and flavours in different cocktail glasses. He handed her a plate. 'Stop. Taste. Enjoy the moment.'

Kelly breathed in and held it. *Enjoy the moment.* When had she last done that?

She frowned. 'I think I've forgotten how.'

When had there last been a moment to stop and enjoy? The day the doctor had stared back at her with a grim face and told her it wasn't good news? The day her hair had started to fall out in clumps?

Or how about the afternoon she'd answered Tim's phone when he'd been in the shower and found a rather graphic text message from another woman? None of those were moments she'd wanted to stop and savour. No, instead she'd powered through them all as fast as she could, closing her eyes and hoping they'd disappear behind her if she ran fast enough.

And she'd never stopped running. The realisation settled over her like a haze.

'Good job you've got me on hand to remind you,' Jason said, and held a miniature cheesecake with a raspberry on top up to her mouth. Kelly stared at it, then took a bite, careful not to accidentally let lips meet fingers.

Heaven. That was the next word to echo round Kelly's head. Pure heaven. She closed her eyes to savour the taste. Eating a New York cheesecake in New York had been on her bucket list, but she'd imagined a little diner somewhere and a waitress in an apron, chewing gum. Never in a million years had she imagined she'd be on the top of the Waldorf, being fed the most exquisite specimen by the best-looking man in the city. The whole experience made her a little giddy.

She opened her eyes to find Jason only inches away. He'd stopped smiling. And she could practically see him vibrating with the same pulse that was pounding in her ears.

'Let's dance,' she heard herself say. 'Do you want to dance?'

She had to do something to break this weird magnetism between them and dancing was supposed to be *fun*, wasn't it?

Without waiting for an answer, or to see what Jason did with the remainder of the cheesecake, she turned away and joined the mass of moving bodies on the dance floor. When Jason joined her he was licking his lips and she guessed exactly where the rest of her teeny dessert had gone. Knowing that if their lips met they'd taste the same sweetness on each other made her insides growl— okay, *purr*—and she wasn't sure it was her stomach doing the talking.

She concentrated on her dancing instead. One thing she'd been really good at once upon a time. However, if she thought she'd be able to scare Jason off or teach him a thing or two, she was wrong. No, Jason was as smooth and effortless on the dance floor as he was everywhere else. He had easy grace and an impeccable sense of rhythm, and Kelly found herself feeling a little jealous to start off with—especially when the girls came flocking and cooing. But he kept his eyes on her, his body turned towards her, and while he didn't ignore the other women, he didn't let them cut in. She was grateful to him for that.

Once she stopped watching him like a hawk, wondering if he was going to disappear with some long-legged, big-boobed model and leave her to fend for herself, she began to enjoy herself. And when Jason took that as encouragement and cracked out some of his more outrageous dance moves, that enjoyment made itself audible. She couldn't remember the last time she'd laughed so much. The weird thing was he didn't look stupid, as a lot of other people would have done, he just looked full of energy, full of life. Kelly couldn't tear her eyes off him.

More than an hour passed and she didn't want to stop moving. Jason was right. This was fun. And when had she last had some guilt-free fun? She didn't have to watch the clock to make sure she was home in time for the babysitter or feel bad she'd missed bedtime stories. It didn't involve counting pennies then putting the item back on the shelf because she didn't really need it and the boys came first. And she was burning calories instead of putting them on. When had she last felt this free?

Before, maybe. She didn't name what. Just *before*. Before everything.

That had been a long time ago.

Almost a different Kelly ago.

So when her chest was heaving and her feet were screaming and Jason asked if she'd like a bit of fresh air, she nodded and followed him towards the long French windows that led to the fairy-lit terrace. The air was cool out there and, eighteen floors below, Park Avenue went about its business. The sounds of taxi horns, the rumble of tyres and the occasional siren made an oddly beautiful serenade.

They walked to one of the lower parts of the crenellated balcony and looked over. Kelly breathed out and turned to Jason. 'Thank you. I think I needed that.'

Jason smiled at her. Not one of his cheeky ones, or his I'm-going-to-get-you-to-do-something-you-don't-want-to-do ones, just a normal, regular smile. Something inside Kelly's chest hiccupped. Jason must have felt it too because his expression became more earnest.

'Why?' he asked softly. 'Why have you forgotten how to have fun?'

She stared back at him. For the first time in her life she didn't want to tell the truth. She didn't want to ruin this moment. This night was all magic and fantasy and glitter. She didn't want to bring it crashing back down to earth by telling him her depressing reality.

But maybe she should.

Maybe she really should.

Before she did something stupid, like believing this could all spin on for ever and she wouldn't get hurt.

He's still Jason, she reminded herself. She couldn't ask him to change and she didn't want him to, but he was not who she needed. Not if she was going to fall for him. And she suddenly wasn't kidding herself anymore that she wouldn't cross that line if they got closer. She'd never been one for holding back and her fragile heart had already latched on too tightly to the man she'd seen beneath the smoke and mirrors.

He stepped forward and looked into her eyes,

tipped his head a little to the side, enquiring. Kelly blocked his image out momentarily with a slow blink, then began. 'My husband left me and our two boys for a much younger—and much bendier—woman,' she said and, Lord bless him, he didn't laugh. He just kept looking at her with that strange un-Jasonlike softness in his eyes.

It didn't work. The truth didn't scare him away like it did other people, so her only option was to plough on, spell the ugly details out fully. 'Right after I was diagnosed with cancer. Lymphoma. It took a load of chemo and a year and a half, but I beat it. So there you have it. Basically, there hasn't been much in my life to find funny recently.'

She could feel her throat growing thick. Odd. She was used to batting these details out to anyone who came too close. Why should this time be any different? Why should the truth she'd waved proudly like a flag catch her out this time?

Jason pressed his lips gently to her forehead then held her close. He didn't move. He didn't say anything. Kelly just breathed in the scent of his aftershave from his jacket and hung on. And then she started to cry. Big, fat tears that made no sound but refused to stop flowing.

How embarrassing.

But he didn't shift uncomfortably after a minute or two. He didn't stop holding or give those little non-verbal signals that Tim had used to give that meant he was finished hugging and was hoping she'd let him go. And Kelly didn't want to let go of Jason.

That was also embarrassing. Because this was not the man to cling to. This was the man to have fun with, and fleeting fun at that. She sniffed and unpeeled herself from him. 'Sorry.'

He shrugged, but that look was still in his eyes and he didn't say anything trite or recite yet another platitude. Kelly was sick of platitudes. The warmth in his blue eyes quickly heated into mischievousness. 'So you've been a little short on good times recently. That just means we've got a lot to pack into the next three days to make up for it.'

She nodded. 'Okay.' There was a bizarre kind of logic to his suggestion. Maybe this trip would help her chill out a little, take life as breezily as she used to. And if there was a man who could teach her to do just that, it was Jason Knight.

They wandered back into the ballroom. The DJ

had put on a slower number and Kelly didn't argue when he took her hand and spun her into his arms.

'Let's start right now,' he whispered into her ear.

Kelly nodded, feeling the solid breadth of his shoulder beneath her head, feeling the sway of their bodies in perfect time. She was too tired to be contrary. Maybe it was the jet lag, or maybe it was just that she hadn't realised how exhausted she was until she'd finally slowed down. It had taken a lot to fight that horrible disease. More than she'd ever let on. And even more to stay whole when Tim had deserted her.

Whole.

She was all better, so that was how she should feel now. But she didn't.

She felt as if the divorce, the cancer, had taken something from her. If only she knew what it was so she could get it back. All she knew was that there was a tiny, nagging hole deep inside.

But she couldn't think too much about that now, not with Jason's warm shoulder under her cheek. Not with his hands resting softly at the back of her waist and her arms flung around his neck, fingers half buried in the ends of his hair.

This. This was what she needed.

To be held without being leant on. To have the space to stop being strong.

To be asked nothing.

And there wasn't anyone more surprised than her that it was Jason giving it to her. Maybe there was magic in this room after all. Maybe they'd shed their protective armour at the coat check on the way in. Because all she knew was that she hadn't felt this close to another soul in a long time. Not physically. Not emotionally. She felt connected to this man in a way she couldn't verbalise, let alone understand. Why him? Why now? And why didn't she care about the answers to either of those questions?

The song changed and the tempo slowed further. Kelly inhaled and then let out a long, shuddering sigh. Jason just pulled her closer. She could feel his breath on her neck, the rasp of his slight stubble on her temple. She didn't have the energy to lift her head from his shoulder and look at him.

The night seemed to stretch on. She didn't know how long they stayed like that. Maybe hours. Maybe only minutes. But, as she stopped fighting the world and just started to *be*, she felt some of her strength returning. Not the kind of strength she'd been existing on for the last few years. Not the make-yourself-do-it strength that was more an act of willpower than anything else. No, suddenly she felt lighter. Stronger. She felt like that winged horse on the ceiling, as if she could jump off the terrace wall and fly. No flapping. No effort. Just the blissful stillness of air beneath her wings and the certainty the warm breeze would take her where she wanted to go. All she had to do was believe and keep her arms outstretched.

If anyone knew that life was too short, it should be her. So why had she been running from it, shutting it out? Why wouldn't she look into the future and hope?

Because *it* was there. The shadow. The threat.

The return of what she feared.

But it might never come. She could stay cancer free the rest of her life. Or she could be hit by a yellow cab tomorrow.

So maybe it was time to remember how to have fun. Maybe it was time to remember how to live.

She slid her hands from behind Jason's neck to his chest. His heart was thudding beneath her palm and the longer her fingers rested there, the faster it beat. She stayed like that for a moment, feeling the warmth of his body against her hand, gathering courage, and then she tilted her face up to look at him.

Somewhere along the way their feet had stopped moving, although she wasn't exactly sure when. He looked back at her. No quick remarks, no flirty comments. She almost wanted him to, because that would make it easier. That would make this a game they were playing, and she feared the stakes might be higher than that. But in the end she didn't care either way. She was going to grab life with both hands again, starting with the delicious man she already had in her clutches. For once she wasn't going to weigh every action up against the thundercloud looming in her future.

She let her lids drift shut, closed the distance between them and found his lips with her own. Jason stayed still. Not frozen, just waiting. Waiting to see if she wanted to change her mind. She didn't.

He tasted so good. Every bit as wonderful as she remembered. Of strength and masculinity with a little bit of danger thrown in for good measure. As she continued to explore his mouth, Jason's hands came up to gently hold her face. Slowly, he joined in with her, till she didn't know who was leading and who was following. It really didn't matter.

Who knew how long they'd have stayed like that, or how far they'd have gone if someone hadn't bumped into Kelly. Her eyes flew open as Jason dragged his lips from hers. For a fraction of a second they stared at each other. Kelly wasn't quite sure exactly what they were saying in tandem. Was it *What the hell was that?* or was it *You too?* Perhaps it was both. Because that hadn't just been a kiss. What they'd shared outside the Tube station had been a kiss. This…this had been *more*. Everything.

And, for some reason, she wasn't as terrified as she should have been at that thought. Her head was telling her it was a very, very bad idea, but deep down inside she couldn't get worked up about it. Her gut told her this was the real him, and her gut was happy with what it saw.

She twisted round to see who had backed into her and found herself staring at Dale McGrath. Jason's hand tightened on her arm.

'Sorry!' she and Dale both said at the same time.

He smiled back at her. 'I reckon that was my fault, seeing as you weren't moving and I wasn't looking where I was headed.'

Kelly gave him a wry look. 'Not sure I was either.'

Dale just grinned back at her, the glow of good humour in his eyes.

'Great party!' she said. 'Thanks so much for inviting us.'

He nodded, but he gave her a questioning look. Before either she or Dale could say anything, Jason thrust out his hand and shook the other man's hand firmly. 'Jason Knight of Aspire Sports,' he said. 'I spoke to your team about our new Mercury running shoes a couple of months ago.'

Dale nodded and where his smile was fading, a frown was beginning to form. Kelly glanced at Jason. Why was McGrath looking at him like that? As if he didn't quite know what to make of Jason. As if he was surprised he was here.

Oh, crap.

Suddenly all the little things that hadn't quite added up all evening made sense.

She wriggled out of Jason's grip and turned to face him, glaring.

'You *crashed* this party?' she asked him in a shrill voice. 'You made *me* crash along with you? What kind of crazy game are you playing?'

CHAPTER TEN

JASON SWUNG ROUND to stare at Kelly. Couldn't she just play along?

Dale McGrath cleared his throat. 'I think I'd like to know the answer to that question. I don't recall seeing your name on my guest list.'

Jason shot Kelly a warning look before turning to face their reluctant host. 'Not strictly...' he began.

McGrath's eyebrows shot up. 'Either your name's there or it isn't.'

Okay. He could turn this around. Jason had talked himself out of tighter spots in the past.

'It isn't,' he said apologetically, hoping the truth would win him a few points. 'But we're staying at the hotel and I took a shot. I know I have a product that you could be excited about, and I was hoping we could set up a meeting to talk about it.'

McGrath looked him up and down. 'You're Brad Knight's brother, aren't you?'

Jason nodded, for once hoping his brother's golden-boy shadow might cast a positive light on him as well. 'Yes, I am.'

'I met him a few times...' McGrath said. 'Solid guy.'

Jason nodded again. That was Brad: solid, steady, worthwhile...all the things Jason wasn't. But this man didn't need to know that.

Their host thought for a moment. 'You've got thirty seconds.'

'Now?' While Jason normally did some of his best thinking on the fly, kissing Kelly had somehow wiped the ability to schmooze and charm away, as if the truth was a virus and she'd now infected him with it too. He was scared of what might come out of his mouth.

McGrath shrugged and narrowed his eyes. 'Take it or leave it.'

Jason knew that face. This guy wasn't joking. He wasn't looking for an angle or making Jason sweat to pay him back for adding himself to the guest list. He knew if he tried to negotiate another meeting that McGrath wouldn't even *politely* return his calls this time around.

The adrenalin started to surge through his veins.

Just like before a race. Jason let it buoy him up, welcomed it in and let it give him his edge. And then he was off and talking, just as if a starter had fired a pistol.

'The Mercury running shoe is a cutting-edge innovation in the field of sports technology,' he said. All that going over facts and figures with Kelly had really helped because, all of a sudden, it was as if he was speaking that brochure aloud. He was schmoozing with actual substance. Cool. 'Obviously, I can't share the exact science of it with you unless you come on board...' He paused to give McGrath his most winning smile.

The other man just folded his arms and shifted his weight back onto his heels.

'But we believe the revolutionary sole and inner design can help shave time off—ow!'

He turned and scowled at Kelly. She'd just elbowed him in the ribs. *Why?*

He turned his attention back to McGrath. 'Can help shave time off the—'

She'd done it again!

'Jason!' She looked at him with desperate, pleading eyes, then looked pointedly at their host, who was losing interest fast.

'What?' he said, not as far under his breath as he'd have liked.

'What are you doing?' she mouthed back.

Pitching his product, that was what. And he'd been doing a pretty good job until his rogue PA had butted in.

'Your girlfriend's right,' McGrath said. 'I've heard a thousand sales pitches just like that. You think you're the first man with a "cutting edge" idea to crash one of my parties and try to sell it to me?'

Jason swallowed. He'd been hoping he was.

'I'm not interested in BS,' he said dismissively, then turned to walk away.

Kelly leapt forward and placed a hand softly on McGrath's arm. Jason scowled at her. There was no way he was going to beg McGrath. If the man was dumb enough to pass him over without listening, then it would be his loss!

'It's not BS,' she said fiercely. 'Mercury really is unique. Jason knows his stuff. He's unconventional, sure, but that means he's got the goods when it comes to knowing how to create something different, something no one else has done before.'

Jason was trying hard to hang on to his anger

with Kelly. She'd managed to stamp all over his one opportunity to sell this idea to McGrath, but he couldn't ignore the warm feeling spreading inside at her words. He might do 'BS', but Kelly didn't. She meant every word of what she'd just said.

McGrath seemed to like it too. The lines on his forehead relaxed and he gave Kelly an enquiring look. 'Unconventional, huh?'

'Yes.' Jason straightened his spine and looked McGrath in the eye.

No one had ever dared call him run-of-the-mill. Reckless and crazy, maybe. But that kind of thinking was what had helped him come up with Mercury in the first place. He'd made the leaps that no one else had thought could be made.

McGrath chuckled. 'I'd say unconventional is about right. Most people try to butter me up before they try to sell me their products. They take me out for fancy lunches, buy me stuff, flatter my wife...'

McGrath's wife was a supermodel and hot as they came, but Jason didn't think that mentioning that now would help him any.

'How long you been here?' McGrath asked, looking around at the party in full swing.

Jason opened his mouth to say *Only a little while*...but Kelly got in first.

'An hour or two.'

McGrath nodded and a slow smile spread across his face. 'You want me to say nice things about your running shoes, but you've crashed my party, danced to my music, eaten my food and drunk my champagne?'

'Pretty much,' Kelly said. Now it was her turn to get an elbow in the ribs.

McGrath just laughed. 'And, from what I saw just now, you two weren't exactly discussing running shoes on the dance floor....'

Kelly flushed bright red.

Jason decided that he'd rather McGrath had continued with his earlier approach—look gruff then throw them out—as he didn't much care for the way the man was playing with them. He could see a couple of security guys near the exit keeping a close eye on them.

'You Brits have a word for it...' McGrath continued, winking at Kelly.

'I think the word you're looking for is *snogging*,' he heard Kelly say beside him, grinning back at McGrath.

If Jason could have dreamt this meeting up in a nightmare it would have been less painful. 'Are you trying to finish me off?'

McGrath slapped him on the shoulder. 'Don't mind her. At least she tells it straight. None of this sidestepping and tap-dancing. Can't stand that.' His expression grew more serious. 'I don't want slick presentations and marketing speak when I consider endorsing a product, Mr Knight. My team can deal with those details. There's only one thing I want to know about—its heart.'

'Heart?' Jason repeated, frowning a little.

'Yup. And that starts and ends with the man or woman behind it.' He nodded at Kelly. 'She's got it. I just don't know if you have.'

Join the queue, Jason thought, but he pasted on his best look of earnest determination. 'Let me try again.'

McGrath grimaced. 'I don't give that many people a full minute.'

'Oh, go on!' Kelly said. 'Otherwise I'll have to snog him again.'

His grim look crumpled into a smile and he turned back to Jason. 'You up for it? But you start with the BS and I'll kick you out.'

This was it. His chance. The one he thought he'd flushed down the toilet five minutes ago. The one he'd been building towards for two years. And he wasn't even allowed to speak his native language. Great.

Jason looked at Kelly, at the close-lipped smile, the bubbling enthusiasm behind her eyes, the way she bobbed in her shoes to keep from letting it all out. How did she do that? How did she bounce back from all she'd been through and literally shine?

He thought of how she'd opened up to him out on the terrace, how she'd told the truth, even though she'd had to dig deep into herself, even though it had cost her so much. He turned to Dale McGrath and opened his mouth.

'I know,' he said. 'I know what it's like to pray in that stillness at the beginning of a race. I know how that starter's pistol sets off a chain reaction you can't control—adrenalin slamming through your system so hard it's all you can do to ride the wave and harness it. I know what it's like to want to win, to reach the finish line first so you can turn around in defiance and shout, "I *am* somebody, and don't you dare forget it!" And that's why I made Mercury shoes, McGrath, for people like you and me who want to make the world sit up and take notice. People who want to win.'

Although the music was still throbbing and people were still dancing all around them, the world seemed to put its brakes on. Around them the room slowed and the noise vanished. All Jason could hear was the beating of his own heart. All he could see was the sceptical look on Dale McGrath's face.

He couldn't quite believe he'd said all that. He looked over at Kelly and her face was aglow with excitement and pride and something else he didn't want to label. She stepped in and kissed his cheek softly.

That was when the world started spinning. That was when the bass beat rumbled through his ribcage once again.

'Pretty words, Knight. Hope your shoes can live up to them.' McGrath reached forward and shook his hand. 'Call my office in the morning and we'll set up a meeting.'

The Empire State Building stood silent and regal before them, its lights steady and unblinking in a cityscape full of movement and noise. Manhattan at midnight was stunning.

It was chilly up on the top of the Rockefeller Center and Kelly pulled her wrap tighter around her shoulders. This was perfect. The only problem with standing on top of the Empire State Building was that you couldn't actually *see* the Empire State Building all lit up—and that was something she'd really wanted to do. She was very grateful to Jason for whisking her into a cab after they'd left the party and bringing her here.

It had been busy when they'd arrived, but now the crowds were thinning and heading back down to the plaza below. It was only because Jason *knew people* that the security guard now standing by the door just nodded and let them stay.

She snuggled into Jason, who was standing close behind her, pointing out the different buildings and telling her a little of their history. He'd lived in this city most of his life and he knew all sorts of interesting little facts she'd never get from a guidebook.

It had been like this since they'd run out of the Starlight Roof laughing. They'd kept in contact any way they could. Simple touches—a hand at her waist, holding on to his sleeve as they hurried for the lift, fingers intertwined in the cab on the way over. Neither of them had said anything, because neither of them had needed to. Something had changed. Deepened. They didn't need to label it. Words wouldn't make it more real.

While he was still talking she turned round, keeping her body close against his, and smiled up at him. 'We did it,' she whispered.

Jason stopped his commentary and looked at her. He'd been pointing in the direction of Madison Square Garden and he now dropped his arm and touched her face, stroking her cheekbone with his thumb.

'Yes, *we* did,' he replied just as softly. 'For the first time I didn't crash under my own steam and see how far "winging it" would get me. And it was all thanks to you.'

She gave him a hangdog look. 'I was more of a hindrance than a help, shooting my mouth off—'

'No,' he said firmly. 'You saved it. He would have blown me off if you hadn't stopped me.'

Her lips curled up even further at the edges. She was so proud of him. 'But you sealed the deal, Jason. Not me. He liked what you said.'

She saw her words sink in and a look of amazement spread across his features. What? Had he thought it had just been luck? A fluke?

He surprised her by picking her up and planting a firm, sweet kiss on her lips before laughing and setting her down again. 'We did it!' he said, shaking his head.

Kelly thumped him on the chest with the flat of her hand. 'That's what I've been trying to tell you!'

His expression grew more serious and he looked into her eyes. 'We make a great team.'

The words caused a shiver to work up from Kelly's core and vibrate its way through her limbs. Jason pulled her tighter and hugged her against him, placing a kiss on the top of her head. She closed her eyes and thought her heart might crack in two.

He was right. They'd worked as a team. Somehow the maverick loner had let her close enough to play with him rather than against him. And she'd played nicely, instead of making up her own rules and insisting on scoring all the goals herself.

This was the man she'd only seen glimpses of in the previous month but had known was there. He was bolder and stronger and just plain more wonderful than she ever could have guessed. And she was falling in love with him, God help her.

The fact she suspected no one else knew this

side of him but her, not his past lovers or even his family, just made her want to weep. She wanted to lean off this balcony and shout it out for the whole city to hear. Make those sirens and car horns stop. Make them listen.

It seemed he must have read her mind because he gave her a look that was deep and passionate and clouded with uncertainty about what was going on between them, but then he kissed her anyway. Kissed her like a man who had nothing left to lose. Like a man who'd flung himself off the cliff and was just waiting to hit the bottom.

A discreet cough from behind them brought them back down to earth. Kelly glanced over Jason's shoulder and gave the burly guard a sheepish smile. He winked back, even as he shivered. She patted Jason's arm. 'Listen, I think we'd better move round and see the rest of the view. That poor man is going to freeze to death otherwise.'

He dropped one last scorching kiss onto her lips then took her hand and led her to look north towards the dark void of Central Park.

She slid an arm around his waist and he lifted his arm and rested it on her shoulder. 'Where are the Knight Corporation's head offices?'

His back muscles stiffened and he said nothing. A few seconds later he lifted his finger and pointed off to their left. When he spoke his voice was light and breezy, just as it had been the first day she'd met him. 'You can't see it from here, but it's just the other side of the Hearst Tower.'

'Jason—'

He pulled her close, pressed an almost absent-minded kiss to her forehead then steered her in the direction of the door. 'You're right: it's cold up here and it's getting late. High time we let the guard get home.'

'You're not going to see your family while you're here, are you?' she asked.

Jason just stared through the taxi window and watched the city go by. 'This trip was a last-minute thing,' he said, still not turning to look at her. 'No time to plan a big, happy reunion.'

She reached for his arm, laid her hand on the sleeve of his jacket. Moments ago, when they'd been on top of the Rockefeller Center, touching had seemed easy and natural. Now the weave of his coat felt rough against her palm and his muscles were stiff under her touch. 'But you're not even going to call, are you?'

He turned and looked at her, gave her that couldn't-care-less expression she knew so well—and hated so much. 'It's no big deal, Kelly. Some families are just like that. We're very independent.'

'Dysfunctional, more like,' she muttered, not so quietly that Jason couldn't hear her. Her family wouldn't win any prizes for sanity and harmony, but at least when it counted they were there for each other. 'It's not going to kill you, you know. Why don't you just call your father, see if he can meet up for a drink—or a coffee? Eight years is a long time. Don't you think you ought to *try* and build a few bridges with him?'

'Leave it,' he told her in a low voice, and the rumble underneath the smooth words told her he was starting to crack. Just like he had that night outside the Tube station. But this time Kelly reckoned he could do with letting it all out. There was no way things were ever going to get better if he kept letting it all fester underneath the surface while he pretended there was nothing wrong. Sometimes the truth just needed to come out.

'Why not, Jason? Tell me. Tell me what the problem is!'

He swung round to face her. 'Why do you think he sent me to London in the first place? Therc's a convenient ocean between us to make sure he doesn't have to bump into me that often.' He shook his head. 'He doesn't *want* to see me, Kelly!'

Usually, her first reaction when somebody attacked was to give as good as she got, but the hurt behind Jason's furious expression drained away any desire to do that. She moved the hand that still rested on his arm just a little, but the cab drew up outside the Waldorf's entrance at that moment and he sprang out of the cab and onto the sidewalk, leaving Kelly's hand to fall onto the cracked imitation leather of the back seat. She sighed and shuffled out after him.

She waited until they'd walked across the lobby, taken the lift to their floor and walked the short distance to their suite. Jason went to pour himself a drink from the bar in the sitting room—bourbon, by the looks of it—and then he walked over to one of the long windows fringed by heavy gold-coloured fabric and stared out through the misty sheer curtain that covered the pane.

'Okay…so things between you and your father are…complicated.'

He gave a short, harsh laugh. 'I never picked you as having that very British talent for understatement.'

She saw the tiny barb for what it was: a distraction technique, one she often used herself, so she decided to let it slide. 'What about your brother? You can't just give up on your family, Jason.'

'Even if they've given up on me?'

She didn't believe that. Her boys could drive her to distraction, but that didn't mean she didn't love them. She was sure it must be the same with Jason's parents, but that Everest-sized chip on his shoulder was stopping him from seeing clearly.

However, the key thing was that Jason obviously believed what he'd said, and she had a feeling he'd never fully conquer that all-consuming need to pull out and not get involved when things got tough unless he faced this. And suddenly Kelly really wanted Jason to be the kind of man who had it in him to stick around, who didn't run from the tough situations in his life.

He downed the last of his drink and put the glass

back down on the sideboard. His gaze flicked towards his bedroom door.

'It's late,' he said and checked his watch, 'and we've had a pretty surreal evening.... I'll see you in the morning.'

She wondered for a moment if he'd kiss her again, but that sense of connection and ease they'd shared not an hour ago seemed to have evaporated entirely. He walked to his room without looking back and she watched him go. When he'd disappeared, she collapsed into the dent in the sofa he'd made and stared at the closed bedroom door.

Great. Just when she'd decided to live a little, take a chance this thing—this rebound fling, or whatever it was—was going to go somewhere, it had all gone pear-shaped yet again. *Great going, Kelly. What are you going to do now?*

CHAPTER ELEVEN

JASON FROZE AT the soft knock on his bedroom door. There was only one person it could be and he wasn't sure he was ready to see her yet. Too many conflicting thoughts were running through his head. He didn't want to say the wrong thing, hurt her, and he was scared he would while he was feeling like this.

'Jason?'

He'd just finished brushing his teeth and the only light still on was the one in the bathroom. Half the room was draped in shadow. He padded over to the door, his pyjama bottoms low on his hips, and opened it.

Kelly was standing there, her hair loose around her shoulders and kinked from where it had been liberated out of its updo. She was no longer in her slinky black dress and red heels, but an over-sized T-shirt that was threatening to slip off one smooth shoulder.

He lifted his chin in lieu of a worded greeting. 'Can I talk to you for a few minutes?'

'Couldn't we do this in the morning...?' he started to say, but she pushed her way past him and walked into his room, leaving him leaning against the door jamb.

'Hey!'

Jason had a surreal out-of-body moment, one where he was looking down on himself, shaking his head, wondering just when he'd turned into the kind of guy who minded when a hot woman beat down his bedroom door.

Kelly walked over to the bed and sat down on the edge. 'I think you need to talk about your family, about your brother's accident.'

Well, Jason thought he had a greater need to jump off the twenty-fifth floor. Didn't mean he was going to do it.

She patted the edge of the bed and gave him a smile that was most un-Kelly-like—shy, sweet, inviting. And bewitching as hell. He found himself walking towards her, sitting down.

But he wasn't going to talk. Oh, no. There were much better games they could play with only a few pieces of clothing between them and a super-king-sized bed as their playing field. He turned to her with a devilish smile and pulled her to him. Her resistance melted a split second after his lips met hers and he gathered the thin cotton of her T-shirt and bunched it in his fists.

This was what he'd been waiting for. Right from the moment she'd first strutted into his office and hypnotised him with that prim top button. But there were no top buttons now, just loose fabric and acres of soft skin beneath. He slid his hand under the hem of her T-shirt, found a long, lean thigh and worked his way up from there. Sweet mercy. He didn't know when he'd wanted a woman more.

Kelly inhaled sharply as his fingers paused at her hip bone, but he didn't stay and explore. Not yet. First rule of play in Jason's bed was that no one quit the game early. There was plenty of fun to be had before the big finish.

'This…this…wasn't what I came in here for…' she gasped.

He knew. That was the point. And he preferred his idea.

His fingers started making lazy circles from her navel up to her ribcage. She arched beneath him. 'Do you want me to stop?' he asked.

Her eyelids were closed and he watched myriad thoughts cross her features. 'Yes…I mean, no…. Oh, God, Jason.'

She pulled him to her and kissed him fiercely. Before he knew it they'd rolled over and she was on top of him. She pushed herself up on her forearms and her T-shirt draped down, offering the most wonderful space between skin and cotton. His fingers resumed their journey and he chuckled deep inside his chest.

Kelly broke away from him, her breath coming in pants. 'This is not funny! I was just going to… I was supposed to…'

'Later,' he whispered, and pulled her back down on top of him for a slow and lazy kiss.

It almost worked. For a while she joined him, teasing him with her tongue, but then she slowed and sat up. 'I know what you're doing,' she told him. 'And it's called playing dirty.'

He put both his hands behind his head and grinned up at her. 'Didn't know there was any other way.'

She didn't smile back. Darn. That kind of line teamed with that kind of smile usually worked for him.

Kelly shuffled up the bed, grabbed one of the pillows and hugged it against her front as she rested back against the headboard. He rolled over and crawled up the bed towards her.

'Jason…' There was both warning and pleading in her tone.

He smiled softly, still pretty confident he could get her to see things his way. 'What, Kelly?'

She kept looking straight into his eyes as he got closer and closer. The curve of Jason's lips increased. She wasn't pushing him away and that had to be a good sign. He paused when they were only inches apart. But as they stayed like that, gazes locked, something changed…melted. The cockiness about the outcome of the evening drained away. Suddenly, all that charm and swagger he'd had planned seemed like a lot of…BS.

That sobered him up pretty quickly.

'I know it would be…amazing…' She blinked slowly and exhaled. 'But I can't be one of your one-night stands, Jason.' She started shaking her head gently and clutched the pillow closer. 'Please don't ask me to.'

Her voice wavered on the last few words and he felt it deep down in his chest, in a place where he never felt anything anymore. The truth worked its way up from that forgotten spot and out of his mouth before he could think about stopping it.

'There's *no way* you're a one-night stand.'

Her eyes shimmered a little, but her mouth tightened. 'How do I know you're not just saying that to get me into bed?'

'You're already in my bed, Kelly,' he said, his tone light and playful, giving away nothing of how much her question had hurt him.

Was this how other people—women—really saw him? A predator with no scruples? He stepped outside of himself for a moment, tried to see himself with their eyes and was ashamed to admit that, yes, a lot of people probably did see him that way. But not Kelly. He hadn't expected that from her. He'd always thought Kelly had seen…more.

His jaw tensed as she continued to stare at him, her eyes making tiny movements as she examined the individual features of his face, searching for the lie—the BS—he realised, and he saw the moment she let out the breath she'd been holding and relaxed her grip on the pillow.

Jason sat back on his haunches and ran a hand

through his hair. 'Boy, that ex-husband of yours really did a number on you, didn't he?'

Her lips crumpled, even though she was still pressing them together, and she nodded.

'You're not a one-night stand,' he told her again. 'You're more than that.'

He could see her doing the math in her head as he reached for the pillow and prised it gently from her grasp before tossing it onto the other side of the bed. She folded her arms back over her torso, hugging herself instead.

How much more? she was thinking. *Two nights? Three? A couple of weeks?*

The truth was that he didn't know, partly because he had no previous experience of how he was feeling right now to help him guess, and partly because he was too much of a coward to look into the future and do the calculation himself. He had a feeling it would be a sum that neither of them could afford.

'Do you believe me?' he asked.

She nodded, but her brows remained dipped over her eyes and her arms locked around her middle.

He knew there was only one way to prove the truth to her. Unfortunately, it did not involve the removal of clothes or further exploration of that creamy, soft skin. He sighed and threw himself onto the other half of the bed. 'Okay,' he said wearily, 'I'll tell you what you want to know, but on one condition...'

'Oh, yeah?'

He checked the display of the digital clock on the nightstand. 'We get *in* the bed.'

Kelly let out a disbelieving laugh, but Jason kept right on talking. 'It's five in the morning London time and we've been running on adrenalin for hours. We're going to crash sooner or later and I'd rather be somewhere comfortable when I do.'

She stared at him long and hard, and then she hitched her legs up and slid them under the covers. Jason slid off the bed, walked over to the bathroom so he could hit the light then made his way back to the bed, allowing the glow of the city coming through the open curtains to guide him. He stretched out, kicking the sheet to one side and was surprised when Kelly scooted closer and tucked herself under his arm. 'So tell me...tell me about your family.'

He turned to look at her. 'You're really going to make me do this, aren't you?'

'If there's one thing the last few years have taught me it's that you can't run from the tough times—you have to turn and fight.'

'Who says I'm running?' he asked, his voice light and unconcerned.

She moved closer and he felt her husky voice warm on his chest. 'Aren't you?'

He put his free hand back behind his head and stared at the ceiling. His mouth began to move, tell the facts. He was surprised how level his tone sounded, like a newscaster delivering a broadcast. 'I was in a foul mood that day. We were on holiday at our villa in Malibu. We'd been there less than a day but my father had me doing laps in the pool, timing me. I really needed a rest, but he started hounding me, lecturing me about my latest race time. I could do better, he said. I just needed to try harder instead of horsing around.'

He heard the smile in her voice. '*Were* you horsing around?'

The careless demeanour cracked a little when one corner of his mouth lifted. 'I did sometimes, but I think what really got me mad was that I was trying my hardest and he just couldn't see it. If anything, I think my training schedule had been too intense, especially as I'd just finished college and I'd worked really hard at my finals. I guess what I really needed was to take a couple of weeks to blow off some steam then come back to it fresh.'

'I suppose he didn't like that idea much?'

'No...' he said slowly. 'Not much. Now that college was done and I wasn't juggling studies with swimming, we were supposed to be moving the professional career up a notch. I'd done well at the world championships that year. No medals or anything, but I was moving slowly up the table and we knew I still had untapped potential. So...my father and I had a huge fight. The biggest we'd probably ever had. And I decided that if he wanted to accuse me of horsing around, I'd show him how it was really done.'

Kelly let out a gasp and covered her mouth with a hand. He guessed she knew him well enough to know just what a dangerous idea that had been.

'We'd vacationed at that villa for years, so I had plenty of similar-minded friends to go and cause trouble with, if I had a mind to. Which I did. Brad begged to come too and, knowing it would make my father mad if I took him along for the ride, I let him. There was a cliff over the sea and we used to dare each other to dive off it—like those guys in Acapulco. There was one spot we used to jump from regularly and no one ever got hurt, but that day my buddies dared me to climb higher to a part of the cliff we'd never had the guts to jump from before.'

He stopped and turned his head to give her a morbid smile. He could just about make out her features in the gloom as she lifted her chin and rested it on his chest, staring back at him.

'You might not believe this, but back then I had a reputation...'

She laughed softly. 'No, really?'

He returned his gaze to the ceiling, unable to maintain eye contact. 'So I did it. I jumped. Guess I was trying to prove something.'

The rhythmic rise and fall of her torso against his paused and he pressed on quickly while he still could. He hadn't told this story in years, but each tiny detail came searing back into his mind like hot metal pins.

'I dislocated my shoulder, tore a bunch of ligaments, but I didn't want to look like a fool in front of my friends so I lied, said I wasn't hurt too bad when really it was all I could do to stay afloat. But then I saw Brad getting ready to jump. I tried to put him off, told him it wasn't for little girls, but he just made rude hand gestures back at me.'

'He jumped anyway?'

Jason nodded. 'He hit the water at an awkward angle and fractured his spine in three places. He was paralysed below the waist.' He shook his head. 'I should have been honest about how badly I'd hurt myself instead of pretending everything was okay. I should have told him the real reason not to jump instead of being a smartass.'

'It was an accident, Jason.'

'Try telling my father that.'

'He blamed you?'

Jason closed his eyes, blocked the darkened room out. 'He had every right to.'

'You didn't *make* Brad jump.'

'I kinda did. I was always teasing him, telling him he'd never live up to his big brother. I should have known he wouldn't have backed down from a challenge.' There was something else he needed to say. Something he'd never admitted to anyone. The words came out hoarse and rusty. 'I blame myself.'

He felt Kelly's hair tickle his chest and he realised it was because she'd lifted her head to press her lips there. A moment later he felt a warm bead of moisture drop onto his skin. He pulled the hand from behind his head and tilted her face upwards with it. He took a moment to stare into her eyes. He could see them glistening in the dull light.

'Don't cry for me,' he told her. 'I don't deserve it.'

He didn't tell her the rest, how he'd sunk into self-pity, dealt with the tragedy as only a spoilt rich kid could—wasting a couple of years and a whole lot of money wandering, doing nothing but getting good and drunk occasionally.

'I'm sorry…I've been angry for too long. Angry at the disease that invaded my body. Angry at my rat of an ex for not being the man I'd believed—no, that I'd *hoped*—he was. The only way I knew how to survive it all was to come out fighting. Sometimes I forget it's okay to stop, and that *fight* makes me say things, do things…' she swallowed '…especially when I care about something. I didn't mean to push you…I just didn't want you to give up.'

'Why?' he asked softly. Why should it matter so much to her?

She sniffed and laid her head back on his chest. 'Boys need their fathers.… I think of my two, how their dad damages them without even realising it when he changes plans at the last minute or when he gets his mum to babysit so he can go out on the weekend instead of spending that precious time with them. I suppose I hoped that if you could mend things with your father that it meant there was always hope….'

He didn't want to tell her the truth—that he didn't think his father would ever forgive him—but it was a different situation with Kelly's ex and his sons. 'Maybe there is.' He even managed to sound convincing, but something else was worrying him, something her gabbled admission had made him think about.

He curled his arm around her and pulled her closer. 'You're okay now, right? All clear?' He kept his voice light, but a chilly whirlpool started up in his stomach.

She nodded. He could feel her cheek moving against his chest and hear her hair swishing faintly.

'Is that how you got through it all? You just kept fighting no matter what?'

'Simple, but it worked. My sister-in-law says the Bradford stubbornness served me well. She says the cancer won't dare to come back.'

There was that word. Cancer. Not something a

person could hide from easily. It sent a shudder right through Jason to know it had invaded the warm body curled up against his. It made him think how fragile life was. And how strong Kelly must have been to defeat it. However, despite all her fighting talk, he'd heard the way her voice had wavered ever so slightly when she'd said it.

'What would you do if it did?'

She didn't hesitate. 'Fight it some more. I don't have a choice. I can't leave my boys on their own.'

She yawned against his chest.

'They're lucky to have someone like you,' he told her. 'Someone who's in their corner no matter what,' he whispered, almost so quietly that she couldn't hear it. 'Anybody would be lucky to have you on their side.'

He was lucky to have her on his side. Because she was. She might tell him when he was being an idiot, but she didn't judge him. She accepted him for who he was, good and bad.

She mumbled something and shifted her weight a little. It wasn't long before the rhythm of her breathing slowed and her limbs, where they were draped across his, grew heavy.

So much for a night of fun.

But Jason realised he didn't mind. The fun could come later. Right now he was content to have her warm body tucked up against his. For the first time in years he didn't feel lonely, and he hadn't even known he'd felt that way until she'd come along and shown him how empty his life had been.

Without her.

Not just plain empty, but empty without *her*.

If a thought like that had rattled round Jason's head a couple of months ago, he'd have drowned it out with a rowdy night out or a hundred laps of the pool. But tonight he didn't feel the usual chill that came when he feared a woman was getting too close, too serious.

Serious. That was an interesting word.

Hadn't Kelly once told him that life sometimes made you take it seriously? At the time he'd thought she'd just been on a rant, but after her revelations tonight he understood exactly what she meant. It came back to that C word. Cancer was not a thing that could be played with.

He sighed. Despite his promises to his HR manager, to Kelly and even to himself, a part of him had still been making a play for her. As the attraction between them had intensified, he hadn't been able to help trying to win her round.

But now that he had her, he didn't know what he was going to do about it.

Usually, he'd have just had the fling, let it run its course, no harm done. But what they were starting to feel for one another definitely went deeper than that, and he knew she felt it too—this sense of connection, this feeling that they didn't need to hide from each other.

He also knew that he didn't want to hurt her. She'd had too much of that already.

The problem was, he didn't know if he had it in him to *not* hurt her, even if he tried. He seemed to have a gift for destroying anyone who came close. Which meant this thing between him and Kelly—it wasn't a game anymore. And he had no idea what his next move should be.

CHAPTER TWELVE

IT HAD BEEN a long time since Kelly had been wrapped up in a man. Years. She'd forgotten how wonderful it felt to have all that strength curled protectively around her, how safe it made her feel, how…not alone. She lifted her head and pressed a silent kiss to Jason's shoulder, careful not to wake him.

She took a moment to study him in the soft morning light. His lashes were long and dark against his cheeks and his mouth was relaxed out of that habitual naughty smirk. Somehow, instead of looking younger and more boyish while he slept, he seemed more solemn, more serious.

She found a huge smile creeping across her face and her insides lifted high and began to soar.

This wasn't going to be just a fling, whatever she and Jason were starting, and she probably should be worried about that. A fling meant short, hot and walking away unscathed. More…? Well, that was a whole different kettle of fish. They wouldn't be able to go back to the office and pretend it was business as usual, that was for sure. Even so, she hesitated to put a proper label on her feelings.

She laid her head back down on his chest and wriggled nearer to him. He made a small sleepy noise and pulled her closer, held her tighter. Kelly closed her eyes and prayed.

What in the world was she going to do?

She knew Jason was far more than the playboy, bad-boy face he showed to the world. He was stronger, more determined. He *cared*. But that didn't mean he didn't have a lot of baggage that was going to make it difficult for him to settle down and commit. Until he worked through all of that, he'd always be tempted to blow everything off and walk away when times got tough. Just as he'd almost done with the Mercury shoes. Just as he'd done with his family.

Just as her ex-husband had done.

And she had two small boys at home who desperately needed stability, who she wouldn't put through the trauma of seeing another man walk out of their life.

She closed her eyes, as if by doing so she could

shut the truth out, and then she stole a few more moments in the warmth of Jason's arms. Then, although it felt as if she were peeling herself away from him both physically and emotionally, she slid out of bed and went back to her own room to get dressed.

Jason stretched his palm and reached out, but all he found were cool sheets and an empty space. Kelly had gone. He rolled over and opened his eyes, took a few minutes to stare at the ceiling.

Well, that was a first. Spending the whole night curled around a woman and no one had gotten naked.

But he seemed to be doing a lot of things for the first time with Kelly. Like talking about things he normally kept buried. Like looking at how much he'd accomplished in the last few years instead of how little. Like not caring that he hadn't made love to her while he'd had the chance.

Not that he didn't want to. Hell, he really wanted to. But there was something different going on there too.

For the first time this wasn't about winning or losing, the ultimate prize being to get a woman into his bed and keep her there as long as he liked—and not much beyond. He wanted that for Kelly instead. He wanted to be with her when she was ready.

He threw the sheet back and got out of bed, then wandered, still in just his pyjama bottoms, into the living room of the suite. Kelly was already there in the tiny but luxurious kitchenette, humming to herself, and the smell of freshly brewed coffee curled towards him and filled his nostrils. She was dressed in her smartest office attire, ready to kick some business butt, but he couldn't help seeing her with her hair loose and slightly tangled and that darn T-shirt slipping off one shoulder.

'Coffee?' she said and smiled at him.

'Please.'

She turned and poured some into a cup. He crossed the room and slid his arms round her middle just as she was replacing the carafe. She paused for a moment, made sure it was securely back in place then turned in the circle of his arms to face him.

She didn't need to say anything. It was written all over her face—the same twisting feeling that was turning him inside out. Was this real or just a strange dream? Perfect or just plain crazy? The beginning of something amazing or just another horrible mistake?

Neither of them knew.

And he understood where the problem lay. With him.

He leant in and kissed her. Softly at first, but it was impossible to keep it that way. Soon all thoughts of coffee while it was still hot were completely forgotten. But he couldn't quite ignore the horrible sense of sadness building inside.

Kelly believed in him—professionally, at least. But she didn't trust him not to break her heart.

And he didn't judge her for that, because neither did he. He wished he could be the man she needed, but he wasn't sure if he had it in him. Maybe one day, but *now*? That was a tall order. And it wouldn't be fair to her to make her wait, or use her as a guinea pig to see if he was ready yet.

The beeping of her phone on the counter interrupted them. Kelly gave him an apologetic smile. 'I set a reminder for nine o'clock so we wouldn't forget to call McGrath's office the moment it opened.'

That was the reason for the trip, of course. So why did he resent that little electronic intrusion?

Kelly stepped out of his embrace and picked up her phone. Jason decided that he'd probably better go and get some clothes on. It was only fair if they were both properly dressed or properly undressed and, with things in their current limbo and a possible business meeting on the horizon, he regretfully acknowledged that the former was the sensible option.

When he emerged from the bedroom, straightening his tie, Kelly was off the phone and wearing a concerned expression.

'What's up? Wasn't McGrath good to his word?'

She shook her head. 'No, it's not that... He's asked us to meet him for brunch tomorrow.'

Jason grinned. 'Well, that's good, isn't it?'

'Yes, of course,' she replied.

He turned and headed back towards his room, loosening his tie. 'Better get out of these clothes, then....'

He could feel the static electricity bristling from her, even though his back was turned.

'Look, I know things got a little...friendly...last night, but that doesn't mean I'm going to strip and come running whenever you call! I have a little pride, you know.' Jason smiled to himself and tugged his tie from round his neck. His grin widened when he heard her mutter, 'I hope....'

He spun round and continued walking backwards in the direction of his room. 'I meant that those aren't the most practical clothes for sightseeing,' he said. 'Your feet will be a mass of blisters if you try it in those shoes.'

'Sightseeing,' she said, frowning, as if she'd never heard of the concept before.

'You said you wanted to see New York. You said you wanted to catch up on lost *fun*. Now's your chance—and with the most charming and knowledgeable guide in the five boroughs.'

She smiled despite herself. 'You're really bigheaded, you know.'

'So I've been told,' he replied. 'But it's not being big-headed if it's true.'

She just shook her head and headed off in the direction of her room. 'Be back in five...no, make that ten,' she yelled over her shoulder.

Jason just smiled and watched her go. They had one day. One day to live in the moment. They could suspend the issues facing them for that long, couldn't they? No promises needed to be made in the next twenty-four hours.

Because there wasn't anything else he wanted to do with this day but be with Kelly and give her the New York adventure she craved.

Breakfast consisted of the fluffiest pancakes imaginable, along with crispy bacon and maple syrup, all washed down with a couple of cups of hot, strong coffee in an old-fashioned diner that was everything she'd imagined a New York diner would be, including the waitress in the apron with her gum and notepad. She must have wondered why Kelly kept smiling at her, as if she was someone famous she'd always wanted to meet. And, in a way, she was. She'd been part of Kelly's unspoken New York dream, and she'd been very happy to know that part had come true.

But as soon as they'd finished eating, Jason had whisked her out of the diner and into a cab and they'd headed downtown. First stop wasn't any of the flashy homes of the investments banks or even Ground Zero but the sidewalk outside an old-fashioned jewellers. Jason grinned as he took in the carved wood and glass Victorian window.

'When I was small my grandfather used to bring me here.' He glanced across at her. 'He was the sort of man who always carried a pocket watch, and every so often his watch—which had belonged to his grandfather—would need some TLC, and he'd bring it here. I always used to think it was the coolest place.'

Kelly raised her eyebrows.

'Because of this....' he said, and pointed to her feet.

Kelly jumped back. She hadn't realised it but she'd been standing on a proper clock, with a white face and ornate black hands, sunken into the side-walk and protected by a layer of thick, scuffed glass.

'That *is* cool!' She shook her head, marvelling at the idea.

Jason shrugged. 'That's New York City for you... always full of surprises.' He reached for her hand. 'Come on, I've got more of its hidden treasures to show you.'

And, before she knew it, they were in another cab, heading towards the Lower East Side. When they got out, she frowned. The neighbourhood wasn't the smartest. Jason led her into a thin community park that must have run blocks and blocks. What kind of treasure could be found here? She really couldn't guess.

But Kelly heard it before she saw it. Birdsong.

And not just the guttural cooing of city pigeons but trills and whistles and arching notes that made her chest squeeze. This tiny fenced-off section of the park was full of ornate bamboo cages, each housing painted-china feeding dishes and a colourful songbird. Larger cages sat on the ground, some with their white-cotton covers still draped over them; some hung from hooks strung on wire between metal posts. About twenty Chinese men, mostly of retirement age, milled around, not really talking to each other but tending to their pets and enjoying the community of like-minded enthusiasts.

The birds were of all different sizes and colours. Some yellow and black, some shades of grey, some earthy green. What should have been a cacophony of different bird calls wove itself into a surprising and ever-changing symphony. It was magical.

'*Hua mei*. Best bird here,' the man standing nearby said, pointing towards his cage. 'Best song. You listen…'

She peered into a cage hung at eye level, and a little brown bird stared back at her. It would have been the plainest of the bunch if not for a shocking blue-and-white outline to its eyes, trailing back from the corners as if it were wearing heavy eye-liner.

The little bird cocked its head, opened its mouth and began to sing. The only thing Kelly could think of doing was to close her eyes and listen. It was the most beautiful thing she'd ever heard. The song was full of chirps and chirrups and changes in pitch and direction. It sang as if its life depended on it, as if it couldn't *not* sing. And the melody almost brought tears to her eyes for that very reason.

This morning, standing here in Sara Delano Roosevelt Park with Jason, was the first time in a long time that she'd felt that same sense of joy at living and breathing. And if Kelly could sing—which she couldn't—she'd have been tempted to throw back her head and trill away with the birds.

'I could stay here all day listening to them,' she said, sighing.

Jason just grinned back at her. 'I had a feeling you'd like it here, but we've got plenty more places to visit before the day is out.' And he slid his hand into hers and laced his fingers between her own.

Kelly looked down at their joined hands and something hiccupped in her chest. This shouldn't feel so right, should it? This shouldn't feel meant to be, as if their hands had been crafted to fit together this way. But she didn't pull her hand from his as they spent almost half an hour wandering round the small sunken garden, listening to each of the birds in turn.

Eventually they ended up back beside the first cage. Kelly felt she needed to say goodbye to this little bird. The owner hadn't been lying—it had the prettiest song of all of them, and she told him so.

'All have unique song,' he told her, 'but they learn from other bird too.' Then he leaned in close and whispered, 'But *hua mei* don't sing if unhappy.'

Kelly smiled softly. 'Then your little bird must be the happiest here.'

He beamed back at her and nodded, and Kelly felt a pang in her chest as they walked away. She'd probably never get to see these birds again or talk to the old man. For some reason that made her incredibly sad.

But she couldn't be sad for too long. Too many amazing things to see—an almost hidden statue of Lenin, of all people, high on the roof of an otherwise-ordinary apartment block, a wander through Greenwich Village, alive with bustling shops and cafés, drinking a pint-sized latte in a little coffee shop, just like in one of her favourite TV shows.

They kept heading north until they reached Central Park. Lunch was a hot dog with mustard—squirted on in a decorative fashion because the vendor liked the look of her, Jason said—and eaten sitting on a rock that poked out of the grass. It was perfect. So was half dozing on the grass, her head in his lap, cloud watching. Who knew that an elephant, a steam locomotive and a baby seal could all be found floating above the Manhattan skyline, completely unnoticed?

He took her up the Empire State Building. Not really a hidden treasure, he said, but still one of his favourite places in the city, even with the crowds on the observation deck elbowing them in the ribs to get a better view or sticking their cameras through the strong wire mesh and trying not to drop them.

They rode on the subway. Not because it was essential to get to their next destination. Just because.

And they finished the afternoon off at the Children's Centre in the public library, staring at the teddy bear inside a glass case that had been the inspiration for Winnie-the-Pooh, along with his battered and only-just-surviving friends. Because her boys might like to hear about it, Jason had said, but he knew the way to the little half-glazed room that housed the display without asking for directions and he smiled at the contents of the case with affection.

'These were favourites of yours, weren't they?' she asked him.

Jason nodded. 'One of the few things my father used to do with Brad and me was take us to the library. We'd always make a beeline for this case before we ran off to choose our books.' He shook his head, still staring hard at the tiny moth-eaten Piglet, who was smiling cheerfully back at him. 'I haven't been here for years....'

That was when Kelly realised what a lot of the destinations on Jason's eclectic list had been about—he hadn't just been showing her interesting and unspoilt areas of his hometown, he'd been showing her *his* New York. The places that held memories for him, even places that held long-denied connections with his family.

That brought a lump to her throat. And an odd ray of hope to her heart.

Maybe. Maybe they could do this. Maybe it wasn't a disaster waiting to happen.

And she so wanted to believe that was true. She didn't want this time in New York to be just a fairy tale. And she didn't want it to end with the cold, grey reality of a London morning as they landed back at Heathrow. Because she wanted to believe there'd been enough of those grey clouds in her past to guarantee she wouldn't meet them again in her future.

She'd paid enough, hadn't she? Surely she could expect some happiness in return.

Jason would never admit to having a case of nerves, but that was what hit him at twenty-five past ten the following morning, just as he and Kelly approached McGrath's chosen meeting spot—a busy diner just off 47th and Broadway.

Just before they walked in the door, Kelly tugged on his hand and pulled him to a stop. 'You look like you're about to poop yourself.'

Jason blinked. There was nothing like the cold, hard truth for making a man feel better.

'But that's what we want,' she added, straightening his tie then kissing the tip of his nose. 'That means it's getting to you. And if it's getting to you, you're good to go.'

He frowned. He was sure there was some kind of backhanded encouragement in there somewhere, but in his current state of agitation he wasn't sure how to dig it out.

'And I'll be there as your wingman.' She smiled brightly at him.

'That's what I'm afraid of,' he muttered as he turned and headed inside.

McGrath and his driver-slash-security guy were sitting in a booth at the back. A waitress led them over to his table. Kelly instantly beamed at the man and accepted his kiss on the cheek with a smile, but Jason felt his bones crunch when Mc-Grath turned his attention to him and shook his hand. *You're not off the hook yet,* the handshake said. *One false move and you're toast.*

Jason's first reaction was to grin and pretend nothing had happened, but he stopped himself. Instead, he squeezed back, not to the bone-fracturing degree of his prospective business associate, but enough to say, *Game on. I'm ready.* To his surprise McGrath nodded and smiled when Jason pulled his hand away and flexed it subtly.

The waitress returned, handed them menus and poured coffee. For some reason Jason was ravenous.

'We'll talk shoes once we've ordered,' McGrath said.

Jason nodded. 'Fine by me.'

McGrath turned his attention to Kelly. 'This your first time in New York?'

She nodded enthusiastically. Jason knew that, in books and songs, writers described people as 'lighting up', but he'd never really believed it was anything more than a pretty turn of phrase. But somehow, when Kelly started telling McGrath about the day they'd had yesterday, she did it. He couldn't take his eyes off her.

When the waitress came back to take their orders, she fell quiet and scoured the menu. McGrath seemed to pay unusual attention to what Jason ordered—a ton of meat with a couple of fried eggs thrown in for good measure.

When the waitress had disappeared again, he looked at Jason. 'Good choice,' he said. 'You can tell a lot about a man by the way he has his eggs. If you'd have ordered one of those egg-white omelettes, you'd have been outta here.'

He must have made a face at the idea of omelettes with no yolks because McGrath almost, *almost*, cracked a smile.

'You've got your ten minutes,' he said. 'Go.'

So Jason went. He told McGrath about the flash of an idea he'd come up with when he'd been investigating the market, how he'd pulled together a team of designers to see if it could be done and how they'd spent the last couple of years making it work. No frills. No fuss. No BS.

He got his ten minutes. And more.

As he finished speaking, Kelly leaned across a little and squeezed his knee. McGrath was less demonstrative, but he wore a smile behind his stony expression.

'I like the idea,' he said. 'I like being in on something from the ground floor. And I like the idea that I'd be first to wear them.' He offered his hand to Jason. 'These Mercuries better be as good as you say they are, Mr Knight, because I'm looking forward to trying a pair on and giving them a road test. If I still like them after that, you've got yourself a deal.'

Jason managed not to pick McGrath up off his feet and spin him round. Just.

He saved it for when he and Kelly were clear of the diner and heading out back towards Broadway. Then he gently let her down again and kissed her as if his life depended on it. Maybe it did. Because he couldn't remember kissing being this phenomenal before. Perhaps because with each touch and taste he was giving, not just taking; he was speaking the truth instead of just making his next move.

He broke away and ignored the raised eyebrows of a few passers-by. 'I want to see more of you when we're back in London,' he blurted out. 'And not just for a couple of dates—that won't be enough...'

Kelly stared back at him. He couldn't tell if she was terrified or overjoyed at his words. And, seeing as he hadn't exactly planned on saying them, he felt pretty much the same way.

He took a breath then dipped his head so it was closer to hers and spoke softly. 'What I'm trying to say is that I want a relationship. With you.'

She was still frozen and staring, which wasn't helping the thudding in his ears. And yet his mouth just kept on moving, saying all sorts of things he was completely unprepared for. 'I...*care* about you, Kelly.'

She lurched forward and kissed him so thoroughly he almost forgot what he'd just said, then she pulled away, shaking her head and laughing. 'Then heaven help us both because the same kind of crazy is creeping up on me too.'

They kissed again, this time softer, slower. The sounds of the city around them melted away.

'I can't believe this is real,' she whispered when they pulled apart. 'I didn't think…'

'Me neither,' he said. 'But I want to try.'

She bit her lip and nodded. 'I do too, Jason, but I'm scared. Really scared.'

The look of pain on her face, even as she smiled sweetly at him, was almost enough to rip him in two. He pulled her close and held her tight. 'I know,' he mumbled into her hair. 'Just give me a chance. I promise I will do my absolute best to be the man you deserve.'

She pulled back and looked at him, studied his face as if all the answers she ever wanted to find might be written there, then after a long minute she nodded. 'Okay,' she said. 'Stuff it. You only live once.'

'Stuff it?' he said, raising his eyebrows. 'Nice. I'm feeling very wanted now….'

She punched him on the arm. 'Shut up and kiss me again,' she commanded him. 'And then you can take me somewhere nice for a late lunch before our flight. Somewhere *really* nice. I think I'm worth it.'

He punched her back. Gently.

But she was. She totally was.

Kelly sang to herself softly as she reached for a bottle and squeezed a good-sized dollop of the hotel's expensive-smelling shower gel into her palm. Warm water hit the back of her head and cascaded down her body in rivulets. She took her time washing. The grime of this city—wonderful as it was—could not be underestimated, and she wanted to smell and look and feel her best for Jason this afternoon. They only had a few hours left now before they headed back to the airport and she was determined to make the most of them.

The shower gel smelled heavenly and her skin was feeling softer already. She worked her way up her legs and then higher, but when she reached her upper torso, she stopped. Her hand remained frozen on her left breast and the water continued to drum on her upper back.

She couldn't move. She couldn't speak. All she could do was stare at the wall, notice the exact width of the grout between the marble tiles.

She closed her eyes and moved her hand over the breast again, slower this time. Firmer. Concentrating on exactly what she could feel under the surface of the skin.

No. Oh, God, no.

CHAPTER THIRTEEN

JASON CHECKED HIS watch. Kelly had gone for a shower more than forty-five minutes ago. He strolled over to her door and listened for running water, but everything was silent. He stood there for a few moments more, but he couldn't even hear her moving around inside.

He knocked gently. 'Kelly?'

Still no sound. He knocked again. 'Are you okay in there?'

His pulse began to skip. Slowly he turned the door handle and pushed the door open. He didn't have to walk more than a couple of feet into the room to find Kelly, still wrapped in a towel, sitting on the end of the bed and staring blankly at the sheer curtain that covered the window.

'What's wrong?' he asked softly.

She didn't react at all as he moved closer and he began to get scared. He'd never seen her like this before. Where was all the life, the movement?

Where was all that *glow* that had captivated him not more than a couple of hours ago?

As he neared her she blinked, shook her head slightly and then looked drowsily at him.

'Kelly, are you sick?'

She blinked again then frowned as she processed his very simple question. 'Maybe... I mean, I'm not...' She paused and cleared her throat. 'Can we just stay here until it's time to leave for the airport?'

He nodded. 'I'll have lunch brought up.'

'Yeah, whatever....' She went back to staring at the window.

Jason's first instinct was to get out of the room. But he made himself stop and look at her again. 'Do you need anything?'

She shook her head.

'Would you rather be left on your own?' She certainly didn't seem to be affected by his presence one way or the other, and someone needed to call room service.

'I think so...'

He'd go then. But not for long. He'd check on her again shortly.

Knowing Kelly's passion for experiencing authentic American cuisine, he ordered a couple of burgers and the hotel's famous salad from the menu. Then he went to pack his suitcase while he waited for the food to arrive. Once he'd tipped the waiter, he knocked on her door again.

She was dressed this time, in casual clothes for the flight back, and she'd moved from the end of the bed and was curled up, clutching a pillow. Her open—empty—suitcase sat on the floor. He walked over and sat down on the mattress next to her. 'It's ready.'

She looked up at him. 'I'll have mine in here.'

He shrugged and stood up. 'Okay...I'll wheel the trolley in. We can picnic.'

She sat up suddenly. 'No.'

Jason froze.

She seemed to realise she'd spoken rather sharply. 'I mean...I'd rather be on my own.'

Now, Jason was used to being on the frosty end of some people's behaviour, and often for good reason, but he couldn't think of one thing he'd done to upset Kelly since they'd got back to the hotel—heck, he'd hardly seen her—and this attitude she was giving him was really starting to tick him off. At least, that was one reason he was starting to feel so agitated. The other was that she was scaring the crap out of him.

He stepped forward again and spoke to her in a firm tone. 'Kelly? Look at me.'

She did. There was a look of shock on her features, as if she couldn't quite believe how she was behaving either.

'You need to tell me what's up.'

Her jaw clenched and she glared at him. He could feel the warmth of her anger radiating out towards him, making his skin prickle. Good. It was better than the lifeless zombie act she'd been pulling.

'Tell me!'

'Okay.' Her voice was tight, defiant. 'But don't blame me if you don't want to hear it.'

'I don't care what it is,' he told her. 'I'm ready.'

Let her tell him it had all been a terrible mistake. Let her tell him she'd rather shoot herself than go out with him once they got back to London. He really didn't care. He just wanted *something* from her.

She scooted further away from him and sat up straight, her back rigid against the headboard. 'I found…' her lip began to wobble '…a lump.'

He frowned. A lump? What kind of lump? On her head? Because that would certainly explain this crazy behaviour.

Her hand flew to her left breast. 'Here…'

That was when the grenade exploded inside Jason's head, when everything he thought he'd known about terror was put into sharp perspective. Suddenly, curling into a ball and pretending to be comatose didn't seem quite so crazy after all.

'Wh…? How…?' He couldn't quite manage to get a sentence out. He stood up and backed away, as if by creating distance he could somehow make the truth of what she'd said smaller and less significant.

'But it could be nothing,' he almost whispered. 'Right?'

She nodded, but she didn't look any happier. 'It also could be *something*. I can't ignore that.'

And neither could he.

Kelly lay on her flattened-out business-class seat with a thin duvet clutched around her. The cabin wall was only inches from her nose and it was all blurry, but she couldn't be bothered to bring it back into focus. Going cross-eyed looking at the wall, maybe even pretending, just a little bit, to be asleep, was much better than making polite conversation with Jason for the next few hours.

Thankfully, the lateness of their flight meant that the cabin lights were off and many passengers were dozing with their eye masks on. Those who were awake were glued to soundless personal TV screens spewing colourful images.

He was saying all the right things, doing all the right things, being attentive and thoughtful. But she just couldn't face him anymore. That was only a thin veil, and behind the veil was the fear. She could see it as clearly as she could see the tiny white flecks in his warm blue irises.

And she knew all about fear. Knew it wasn't logical or tame. Knew it sprung from somewhere deep inside that couldn't be controlled by conscious thought. This kind of fear was a reflex. Fight or flight.

She knew what she'd chosen—fight. She had to.

But she also knew Jason's ingrained reaction lay down the other path.

And that was what she really couldn't face. It was breaking her heart.

Jason picked up Kelly's case from the baggage carousel and dumped it onto the waiting trolley. The flight in had been strange. Kelly had flattened her seat out once the seat-belt sign had gone off and just laid there for an hour. Then she'd sat up and seemed more normal. *Seemed* more normal.

She'd eaten a meal, watched a movie, slept a little. She'd even said a handful of sentences to him. Bland, functional words, sure, but at least she'd left the catatonic state behind. She seemed to be calm and together. Dealing with things.

Maybe she was.

Or maybe she was freaking out inside and this was the only way to cope. He knew that was what he was doing. The urge to just pretend it was all a bad dream was becoming almost irresistible.

So he gave her room, let her have the thinking space she needed. She'd bounce back sooner or later, wouldn't she? She'd start fighting, the way she'd said she would. And it wasn't until Jason watched her walking, poker straight, in front of the trolley that he realised how much he needed her to do that.

As they went through the doors to the arrivals hall he called out to her, 'I've got a car waiting.'

But at the same moment he saw her lift her hand and wave half-heartedly at someone on the other side of the barrier. An unreasonable and scorching jealousy poker seared through him, thinking it might be her ex-husband. But he saw an attractive blonde rush towards her and a tall guy scowling at him. The expression on his face was completely familiar to Jason; there was no doubt that this man was her brother and he seemed to be holding Jason personally responsible for something.

His jaw tightened and he met the man's gaze. For once in his life, he'd been anything *but* trouble to a woman. You'd think he'd get some kudos for that, at least.

Kelly looked over her shoulder at him. 'Thanks, but I arranged transport.' And then she looked away again.

Transport. Was that all he was now? *Transport?* He pushed the trolley faster to catch up with her.

'Kelly!'

She stopped walking, paused for a moment, then faced him. For the first time since she'd zoned out on the plane there was emotion in her expression. Her eyes glimmered and when she spoke it was a hoarse whisper. 'Jason, I…' She shook her head. 'Please…I'll see you on Monday.' And then she stepped in close and softly kissed his cheek before turning away and heading into the arms of the blonde for a long hug.

The brother came and retrieved her case from the trolley, still keeping a beady cyc on Jason, and then he was left standing there on his own, people from the next flight streaming around him as he watched them leave the terminal.

'How are you holding up?'

Kelly took a moment before she responded to her sister-in-law. She'd been listening to the drumming of the rain on their conservatory roof and it had momentarily helped her to zone out.

'As well as can be expected,' she told Chloe. 'Seeing as I've got another week before I can attend the clinic for tests.' She reached over the kitchen table and squeezed her sister-in-law's hand. 'Thanks for inviting me for lunch.'

Chloe smiled. 'You know you and the boys are always welcome, and I love any excuse to cook a huge Sunday roast...'

Kelly frowned. 'It sounds as if there's a *but* missing at the end of that sentence.'

The smile faded from Chloe's face. 'I suppose I wasn't sure you'd come, although I'm glad you did.'

Kelly couldn't help laughing. 'Why wouldn't I come? I didn't have to cook and you saved me from being cooped up indoors in this horrendous, supposed-to-be-summer weather with the boys bouncing off the walls.' Her expression grew more serious and she swallowed. 'I'd have ended up getting fractious and shouting at them, and they really don't deserve that.'

'No...' Chloe agreed. 'I'm just glad you're letting me and Dan help, in whatever small way we can, that's all.'

Kelly's eyebrows hitched. 'Are you saying I'm normally some antisocial grouch who won't even accept free food when it's on offer?'

Chloe shook her head. 'Don't be daft. I just meant that sometimes you put up some pretty thick walls.'

'Last week you told me I'm the most open person you know.'

Chloe stood up and went to check on the dinner. She opened the oven door and a waft of chickeny steam escaped. Moments later it hit Kelly in the nostrils and her stomach contracted in hunger.

'It's not the same thing and you know it.' She gave Kelly a hard stare as she looped the oven gloves back over the handle on the door. 'There's a difference between saying the first thing that comes into your head and being…guarded.'

'I'm not guarded,' Kelly said quietly. At least, she wasn't anymore. She felt as if all those thick walls Chloe had accused her of having had crumbled into ash. She kept trying to gather them to herself, find some kind of refuge in them, but they disintegrated under her touch.

She shook her head and a single tear slid down her cheek. 'I'm scared, Chloe. And I'm doing my best not to be, but I don't know if I can do it all again!'

Chloe rushed over and put her arm round her. 'It could be nothing… You said that yourself.'

Kelly nodded. Yes, she knew what she'd said. But wishing wouldn't make it true.

'But if it isn't…'

'You can't think like that!'

Chloe sounded almost angry. Kelly wished she could summon up some of that fire herself. She needed it. For so long she'd lived with it burning away inside her and now, when it could really do some good, it had flickered out and died.

'I know, I know….'

At that moment, her three-year-old came running into the room. He made a beeline for Kelly and launched himself at her. She hauled him into her lap and hugged him tight. He hid his face in her shoulder and only peeked out again when Dan came storming into the room. She hauled in some oxygen. She couldn't be weak now, she couldn't. She'd have to find that fire from somewhere. Find that fight.

And she could only think of one way to do that. Only one area of her life had changed.... Her boys needed her to be strong and she wouldn't let them down.

She smoothed back Ben's hair and kissed his forehead, made herself look and sound like the mother he recognised.

Dan brandished a red felt-tip pen. 'I just found him with this,' he told them, 'and a guilty look on his face.'

Kelly's insides dived and she looked down at her son. He'd been drawing on the wall? Again?

'You'd just better hope I got to him before he went all Picasso on us,' Dan said. 'I'm going to check the downstairs cloakroom, seeing as that was the location of his last masterpiece.' He stomped from the room.

Kelly shot Chloe an apologetic look, but held her son tighter. She knew she was supposed to discipline him at this moment, but now she was hugging him she couldn't seem to stop. 'I'll repair the damage, if there is any.'

Chloe just looked heavenwards and let out a breath. 'Ignore my husband. He knows perfectly well we repainted with washable paint and that pen will probably come off with a bit of elbow grease and a damp cloth.'

'Ben?' Her son looked up at her with unblinking, innocent eyes. Kelly stared back at him. She knew that look. He was going to be in big trouble when his uncle found where he'd decided to explore his artistic skills. She picked him up and set him on the floor, even though he tried to cling to her. 'You'd better go and show Uncle Dan where you did the drawing.'

Ben bit his lip and shook his head.

'The longer he spends looking the angrier he'll be!'

Ben ran off in the direction of the lounge. Kelly closed her eyes and prayed that Chloe's cream sofa was still as pristine as it had been when they'd arrived, then she turned to look at her sister-in-law. 'What's got my brother in such a grump today?'

Chloe sighed. 'Aside from the fact the weather gods decreed he shalt not barbecue?'

Kelly nodded. Dan had lightened up a ton since he'd met Chloe. This bear-with-a-sore-head routine was reminding her of the 'old' him.

'We had another argument about having a baby. He says it's too soon, my mother says I'm almost too late and I...' her eyes misted over '...I just want one so badly it hurts.'

Kelly nodded, even as the back of her nose started to feel thick and her eyes prickled. 'You just leave him to me,' she said with a grim face. 'I'll put him straight.'

Maybe *after* Ben's latest artwork was found and erased, though. There was no point looking for trouble.

Jason arrived while the cleaning staff were still doing their rounds on Monday morning. Although dawn had been hours ago, London looked as grey and damp as it usually did on a winter afternoon.

He had to see Kelly at the earliest opportunity to know if she was okay. He'd sensed she needed space—from him, as well as everything else, unfortunately—and he'd given it to her, even though it had been agony.

After the accident that had changed his and Brad's lives, people had flurried around him, saying the most inane things, as if their paltry attempts at cheering him up could make a difference. He'd wanted to tune them all out. And he'd learnt to. He'd learnt how to pull back inside himself and find space to heal on his own terms, and he'd showed Kelly the same respect by allowing her to do the same.

Didn't mean he didn't want to see her, though. Didn't mean he wasn't waiting for that moment when she'd burst through the office door, wiggle her way over to his desk, give him one of her long, flesh-stripping looks then open her mouth and finish the job with a choice phrase or two.

When he heard movement in the outer office, he couldn't help himself. He rushed across his office and flung the door open. She was taking her raincoat off, shaking the drips off the shoulders before hanging it up, and he didn't think he'd ever seen her look more beautiful. Gone was the casual travel wear of the previous Friday, replaced by her favourite pencil skirt and the same blouse she'd worn the first day they'd met.

He didn't waste any time in closing the distance between them, but as he pulled her close, pressed his lips to the little space under her ear, Kelly went still in his arms.

'Jason,' she said in a warning voice. 'Not here.'

He looked up and realised what she meant. The door to the ante-office was open and anyone walking past could have seen them. He ran his hand down her arm to catch her fingertips and then tugged her in the direction of his office. With two sturdy closed doors between them and the outside world, they could make up for lost time.

But Kelly slid her fingers out of his, then tidied an invisible strand of hair by tucking it behind her ear. 'Give me a moment, will you? I'll be right in.'

He nodded and backed up to his office door, not quite able to tear his eyes off her and look away. She looked well, didn't she? And the greyness of whatever mood had settled on her on their return flight had gone. That had to be a good sign.

So he went back into his office and waited, resting his butt against the desk and crossing one foot over the other. Moments later Kelly appeared, pad in hand and walked towards him. She stopped when she was just out of touching distance. Jason deposited his weight back on his feet so he could rectify that.

Kelly folded her arms, hugging her notebook to her chest. 'I…I don't think we should get too…you know…at the office. People will talk.'

Frankly, Jason didn't care if his staff wrote a musical about them and performed it on the street in front of the building. In fact, he might just audition for the role of leading man himself.

He let one side of his mouth hitch up. 'One little kiss won't hurt.'

Kelly glanced nervously over her shoulder at the closed door. That didn't stop him from moving closer, from tugging the notebook and pen from her stiff fingers and throwing them onto the desk behind him. It also didn't stop him sliding his arms around her and teasing her soft lips with his own. She closed her eyes and let out a jagged sigh.

This was better. This was what he'd been dreaming about all weekend. Well, *part* of what he'd been dreaming about all weekend. The full-length version had a lot more skin-to-skin contact and nowhere near as many clothes.

She allowed him to kiss her and then she placed a hand on his chest and stepped back. 'Not a word all weekend and now you're all over me?' Funnily enough, she didn't seem to be angry. 'I thought I'd scared you off.'

Ah, there it was. The hint of challenge in those last words, the tiny flash of something hot behind her placid expression.

'No,' he said. 'You know that's not true.'

She raised her eyebrows. 'Do I?'

Yes, she did. She knew him better than that. He gave her a look that told her as much. She looked away.

'Whatever it was we were starting, Jason…I think we should put it on hold.'

He blinked. The words made no sense to him, not at first. It took a while for them to shuffle themselves into the right order and sink in. 'On hold?' What did that mean?

She crossed her arms again and shot him a plead-ing look. 'I don't know what's in my immediate future, let alone the long term.' She broke eye con-tact and stared at her shoes before looking at him from under her lashes. 'I need to concentrate on me and my boys at the moment. It's just not the right time for a relationship…or whatever.'

Or whatever.

Jason didn't lose his temper very often, too busy floating above any negative emotions for them to have any impact, but now he could feel his blood pressure climbing.

Or whatever?

Even his father had never damned him with such faint praise.

'I'm not saying for ever. Just for now. I can't… deal…with it right now. I've got too much else on my mind.'

And now he was a problem to be dealt with. *That* sounded like something his father would say. He'd just never thought he'd hear those kind of words coming out of Kelly's mouth. She might tell it straight, but she was never usually that hard and judgemental.

He shook his head, walked back around his desk and sat down in his chair. 'Fine,' he said, his voice taut. 'Whatever you want.' And he picked up his basketball and shot it through the hoop without even lining it up.

CHAPTER FOURTEEN

THE BASKETBALL ROLLED across the floor. Kelly watched it for a few moments then walked stiffly to pick it up before handing it back to Jason. 'This has all happened so fast. It's all so new. *Too* new.'

Too new for all she might have to face in the coming months. She didn't even know if she had the strength to cope with it. Maybe because she understood what was coming. Jason might have good intentions, but he was clueless. She didn't want to lean on him, trust him, then find it was all too much and she was on her own again, worse off than she would have been if she'd been standing on her own two feet.

She knew he was angry with her, but she had to make him see.

'You haven't thought this through,' she told him. 'If the tests come back positive, there'll be chemo or radiation treatment—quite possibly surgery. I'll be ill all the time, no energy to do anything. Not much fun in that. And, if it is the worst-case scenario, my chances of surviving and living a long and happy life might be slim. All treatment can do is extend the time I have left. Can you really handle that?'

She'd never seen Jason look so serious. He was completely still, staring back at her, and she watched the colour drain from his face. 'Maybe.'

Maybe wasn't good enough. Not now.

A few days ago she'd have taken *maybe* and run with it, but things had changed.

'And what if I let you into my life? How close are we going to get? Are you going to move in and look after me when I'm throwing up and my hair is falling out in handfuls? Are you going to want me if I only have scar tissue where I once used to have breasts?'

She knew these were hard truths, but if he really wanted to be with her he was going to have to deal with them.

'Will you take on my boys if one day I'm not here anymore?'

He opened his mouth and shut it again.

That was what she'd thought.

He shook his head, rested his elbows on his desk and put his head in his hands. A second later his whole body shuddered, and her heart went out to him. It wasn't his fault. It wasn't anyone's fault. But he had to understand what he was asking her to gamble and why it was too much.

He peeled his hands from his face and looked up at her. 'But I'm falling in love with you.'

Kelly closed her eyes. The hits just kept on coming. And here was another one: she knew the moment the words came out of his mouth that she could reply in kind. But it wasn't enough. Cancer killed more than bodies; it killed relationships, hope, dreams. She and Jason would become just another set of casualties.

She walked over to him, slid onto his lap, put her arms round him and rested her forehead against his. Then she kissed him, slowly and sweetly, all the while feeling tears threaten at the backs of her eyes. 'Thank you,' she whispered. 'Thank you for wanting to do this....'

He pulled her closer until their bodies were crushed against each other's. 'You don't know anything for sure yet.' He moved his head back to look at her. 'Let me in, Kelly. Let me try...'

The earnestness in his eyes was more than she could handle. A tear slid down each cheek.

'Maybe,' she said hoarsely. 'Maybe when the tests are done, if everything is looking good…'

But she knew she was lying. This was the kiss of death to whatever had started between them. There'd be no going back afterwards. Even though she understood how much of a step this was for him, a small part of her would always resent him for not being able to step up to the plate when the time had come. A larger part would fear for what would happen if he was faced with the same dilemma in the future.

He sighed. 'Okay…good.' And then he lifted her off his lap and set her on her feet. 'But we've got a lot to do this week if we're really going to knock McGrath's socks off with our shoes. We can't spend all day necking in my office chair.' He smiled at her, his usual nothing-touches-me smile, but there was a dullness in his eyes and a tightness in his jaw. Kelly's stomach rolled.

He knew she was lying too.

Jason slid into the lukewarm water, welcoming the familiar smell of chlorine, and began to swim. This was his fourth time in the pool this week and it was only Thursday morning. That was a hell of a lot of thinking he'd had to do, and he still hadn't come up with any answers.

During those countless laps he'd thought a lot about what Kelly had said to him on Monday morning. He hadn't been able to give her a definitive *yes* when she'd flung all those hard questions at him but, the more he thought about it, the more he wondered if anyone would have been able to give her the words she wanted. It had been a lot to deal with in one go. Like a cannon blast to the chest. No wonder he'd wobbled. That had definitely not been the moment for a quick, breezy, *Sure! It'll be fine!* Those were some serious questions she'd asked him.

And she'd chickened out of giving him the time to seriously consider them.

He reached the far end of the pool, performed an effortless turn and relished the way his muscles knew exactly what to do, how natural it still was, even after all these years. This had always been his refuge when the people around him started driving him crazy. Swimming was pure, delightful simplicity.

He rolled over and changed to the backstroke, keeping his focus on the large fluorescent lights suspended from the ceiling on chains. His mind drifted back to Brad, to his father, to the accident. It had done that a lot while he'd been swimming this week and he wasn't sure why. What had that to do with Kelly and the mess he found himself in right now?

But, as he continued to swim, lap after lap, stroke after stroke, things began to sort themselves into an order inside his head. He started to be able to look back on his twenty-two-year-old self and work out what made him tick, how he'd coped with the guilt and pain his dumb stunt had caused. Or, how he hadn't coped with it. How it had been too much to deal with so he'd just…checked out.

He'd taken a step back from life, from his relationships, from caring about anything. And maybe that had been selfish, but it had also been the only way he could claw his way through it. And he couldn't bring himself to say he'd been wrong. Kelly had done the same thing after finding that lump in the shower. It was a natural reaction—to flinch away from the thing that hurt you.

He slowed his pace and changed to the breaststroke, needed the slower rhythm to help his thinking.

But a flinch was supposed to be a momentary

thing—not a lifestyle. No, his mistake had been that he'd never checked back *in* again. He'd chosen to live his life on the margins, and now he looked back on a decade he'd *thought* had been filled with carefree fun and good times and saw nothing but alienation and emptiness.

He put his feet down and stood on the bottom of the pool, then he walked to the edge and used his arms to haul himself out of the water in one fluid motion. As he headed for the changing rooms, one of the swimming coaches for the kids' classes sidled up to him. 'You're really good,' she said. She might have even batted her lashes a little bit, but Jason didn't really notice. 'You should be a pro.'

Jason nodded absently and carried on his way.

Yes, maybe he should be a pro. But that was just another thing to add to the list of things he should be.

And top of that list?

He should be with Kelly.

He arrived at the office half an hour later with his hair still damp and the faint, and not altogether unpleasant, sting of chlorine in his eyes. Kelly was nowhere to be seen, but a quick check of his smart phone revealed she was running late due to child-care issues. He texted back and told her to take the rest of the day off. She could probably do with the break, and he knew he could too.

On the surface everything was fine. They were polite, professional, grown-up.

He and Kelly were boss and PA again, working as a team, and everything was going smoothly on that front. But there were no more fireworks in the office. They were being nice to each other, and they'd never been *nice* to each other. He hated it.

He opened his office door to find Julie sitting in his chair behind his desk, a crisp white envelope in her hand. She didn't look very pleased to see him.

She stood up, slapped the envelope down on the oak surface and crossed her arms.

Really? Again?

'Julie…' he began.

She shook her head. 'You knew the deal and you decided you couldn't keep it in your trousers.'

Jason's mouth dropped open. Not because of how his HR manager had spoken to him, but because he really hadn't dated anyone at work since their last conversation.

'You're wrong,' he said, not even pretending to

look sheepish. She wanted a fight? Well, he'd give her a fight! Turned out he was just in the mood.

'Oh, yes? Then why was your PA down in my office yesterday afternoon, trying to subtly ask— and failing, I might add—to be moved to another department?'

Jason must have looked as dumbfounded as he felt because Julie cocked her head to one side and studied his reaction closely.

'I don't know why she came to see you,' he said. 'But it is categorically *not* because I slept with her.' Not for want of trying on at least a couple of occasions, but no point telling Julie that now.

She narrowed her eyes. 'Then why has Kelly got that look?'

He didn't know what she was talking about. 'What look?'

And Kelly wanted to leave him? To move to another department? The thought made him sick. Not just because he wouldn't see her every day anymore but because it surely didn't bode well for any future relationship. She was already pulling away. Something deep down inside started to ache.

Crap. *This* was why he didn't like to care about anything. Because it hurt so freakin' much!

Julie snorted. 'I've seen enough of your casualties to recognise it, believe me, so don't you try and tell me...' She trailed off mid-sentence and just stared at him, her eyes widening.

'You too?' she said, shaking her head. 'It's finally happened, hasn't it?'

Jason couldn't do anything but let out a couple of pints of air and then nod his head.

Julie's arms fell by her sides. 'And it's got you good, by the looks of it!'

He just sighed and looked at his shoes. He didn't *do* conversations about feelings, especially not with a woman half the staff thought was a flesh-eating robot.

She stood up and walked over to him, laid a hand on his arm. 'So why do the two of you look as if the world's about to end if you both feel the same way?'

He kept his head bowed but twisted it to look at her. 'It's complicated.'

Julie gave him a half-smile. 'It always is, sweetheart. Don't ever believe it won't be, but it's worth it.' She lowered her voice. 'And *is* she worth it?'

Jason closed his eyes. There was this odd tight feeling behind them that was most uncomfortable.

'Yes,' he whispered. She was worth everything. With difficulty, he opened his eyes again and focused on Julie. 'But you know my track record better than anyone. I think it's scared her off. But I've changed, Julie, really I have.'

Her smile spread to the other side of her mouth too. 'Yes, I think you might have.' And then she withdrew the hand that had been gently resting on his forearm and used it to punch him in the bicep.

'Ow.'

Julie just chuckled. 'So *prove* you've changed. Do something that'll leave her in no doubt. You're a smart guy... You'll come up with something.'

And then she collected her envelope from his desk, tucked it into her pocket and walked towards the door.

Jason hadn't seen this view for at least three years, but here he was, standing on the twenty-fifth floor, staring out across the Manhattan skyline, the Hearst Tower looming large off to the right. Five minutes, his father's PA had said. Jason wondered if dear old Dad would make him wait ten before he let him in.

Much to his surprise, the door to his father's office opened after three. Jason turned from where he'd been staring out of the window, ready to see the look of complete indifference in the man's eyes. His father wasn't one for effusive demonstrations. Anything above a frown would probably be considered a warm welcome.

Jefferson Knight nodded at his son and indicated for him to enter his domain. 'It's been a long time, Jason.' He paused a moment and the threat of a scowl pinched his features. 'Everything is all right at Aspire, I hope?'

'Everything is fine,' Jason said lightly, and sat down in a comfortable leather chair without waiting to be asked. 'In fact, it's more than all right. Dale McGrath is ready to sign on the dotted line to endorse the Mercury shoe line.'

His father had been preparing to sit in his office chair, but he paused momentarily before allowing his butt to hit the seat. 'Really? I'd heard he knocked you back.'

Jason shrugged. 'I talked him round.'

The edges of his father's eyes crinkled just slightly. 'That's quite a coup.'

Jason had waited years to see that look. It was the same look he wore when Brad finished well in a race or he saw a story about him in the paper. But somehow he didn't feel jubilant he'd finally proved the old man wrong, that 'the look' was finally directed at him. All he felt was hollow and empty. And he hadn't told his father the whole truth, either.

'Actually, I couldn't have done it without the help of my new PA. She's turning out to be quite an asset, even though she's only temping for us at present.'

His father pressed his palms together and spread his fingers. 'Then I hope you're going to make her position permanent. The company is nothing without the people behind it, Jason. I've always told you that.'

He nodded. Partly because, after a few years of heading up a business himself, Jason suddenly understood the wisdom of his father's much-repeated expression, and partly because he was sidestepping telling him that he probably wouldn't offer Kelly a permanent position. Not unless things changed. He had a feeling she wouldn't accept, even if he did.

Stupid thing number one he wasn't going to own up to. How many more was he going to chalk up before the meeting was over?

His father leant back in his chair and regarded him carefully. 'You didn't come all this way to tell me about Dale McGrath,' he said. 'What's really on your mind?'

Jason swallowed. As always, his father didn't miss a trick. Of course, he'd have expected his son to trumpet his success in an email or a glossy report his father could pass out to the shareholders. When had Jason last delivered a piece of good news in person? Man to man. Because that was what they were now, he realised, not omnipotent parent and approval-seeking child.

He looked down at his hands, which were resting casually in his lap. 'I wanted to apologise, Dad. For a lot of things…For not making the time to see you and Mom when I've been in the city.' He looked up to check his father's expression. The older man had gone very still and his grey-blue eyes were fixed intently on his son. 'I'm sorry that I haven't always been the son you've wanted me to be, that it's taken me a long time to learn some hard lessons.'

'Jason…'

'No, Dad. Let me finish.' He inhaled and looked his father in the eye. 'Most of all I'm sorry for what happened to Brad—for what *I* did to Brad—and for how it tore our family apart.'

His father nodded slowly. 'Thank you for saying that, Jason. I've been waiting a long time to hear it.'

Jason exhaled. He'd never said it before, had he? Had never shown any true remorse to his family. At first he'd been too busy soaking in self-pity, and after that too busy fooling the world he didn't care. How had he been so thoughtless and so shallow? No wonder his father despised him.

He uncrossed his legs and sat up a little straighter in the chair.

His father stared back at him for what seemed like an age. Well, what had he been expecting? That his father would pull him into a bear hug and tell him all was forgiven? At least he'd said what he'd come here to say. At least he'd started the process of reconciliation. How far they got down that road wouldn't only be up to him.

But then his father lifted his chin and spoke again. 'You're right. I haven't always been proud of some of the choices you've made. You have a way of pushing against any kind of authority that makes it very difficult to get close, and I know you've sensed that I found it easier to get along with your brother than I have with you.'

Jason couldn't find the words to respond. From his father's lips that was almost both an apology *and* an admission of guilt.

'But you've proved me wrong and done well with Aspire,' his father continued. 'And I appreciate you coming and talking to me face to face, saying what you've said. It can't have been easy…'

'Maybe this can be a fresh start,' Jason said and, as he did so, he thought of Kelly. This development, as well as the McGrath deal, was down to her too. He wished she was here with him. He'd have loved to see her butt heads with the stubborn old goat. He reckoned his father would like Kelly. A lot.

His father picked up his phone and dialled. 'Then I'd better call your mother,' he said. 'If she finds out you've been to see me and I didn't invite you for dinner, neither of our lives will be worth living.'

And then he smiled. He actually smiled.

Jason couldn't help grinning back.

Jason had disappeared from the office on Friday at lunchtime and if Kelly had thought not having to see him every day, not having to pretend everything was fine and dandy when she was really aching to touch him would be easier, then she was wrong. She hated herself for being so weak.

You've got to get over this, girl, she told herself. You need all your strength for Monday when you go to the hospital for the first round of tests. You can't let him sap you like this.

She swore out loud, realising she'd happily told the computer, no, she didn't want to save the document she'd been working on all afternoon. Damn Jason. Damn, damn Jason!

Kelly sighed and rested one elbow on her desk and dropped her head onto her hand. It really wasn't Jason's fault she'd fallen for him. He hadn't done anything—apart from being sexy and funny and amazing, of course.

God, men! They were always doing the opposite of what you wanted them to. Want them to stay and they leave. Want them to be a good father and they could only be a crappy one. Want them to be the perfect, no strings, rebound fling and they go and break your heart! It so wasn't fair.

She shook her head and stared at her computer screen. The little clock in the corner said it was only just past three. Her boss had disappeared off to heaven knew where. She was going home. And if she got fired, that'd be the least of her worries. She could pick the boys up early and Chloe could claw some of her afternoon back for herself.

When she got to Chloe and Dan's she discovered that her brother was also home and messing around in the greenhouse he kept at the bottom of the garden. Kelly was still fired up about the stupidity of the male species in general, so she decided she might as well put it to good use. She marched down the lawn and stepped into the sweltering heat of the eight-by-ten glass structure.

Dan turned round, took one look at his sister's face and sighed. 'What now?'

'You're being a pig-headed wally,' she told him.

He blinked. 'Don't hold back, sis. Tell me how you really feel.'

She glowered at him. 'You've got an amazing woman back there,' she said, jerking her thumb at the house. 'And you're making her really unhappy.'

Dan's expression became stony. 'What goes on between me and my wife is none of your business.'

'You're shutting her out!' she said in exasperation. 'I know you're scared witless—hell, we're all scared of something—but at least share that with her. Let her help you. That's what people who love each other are supposed to do.'

He raised his eyebrows and tipped his head to one side. 'Really? You want to go there?'

'Oh, shut up,' she told him. Why did her stupid brother have to pick right now to start making sense?

She sighed and shook her head. 'Just talk to her, will you? Tell her how you're feeling, admit that you're scared. She'll understand that after a cot death any parent would be scared to try again, but you can't stop living your life, doing what makes you happy just because there's the possibility of something bad happening...' She trailed off. 'Oh...'

'Yes, *oh...*' Dan said and turned his attention back to the straggly little plant he was trying to pot. 'That's the thing about greenhouses... Stone-throwing is a hazardous pastime.'

CHAPTER FIFTEEN

IT WAS A nice-enough waiting area, as hospital waiting areas went. Pale green chairs in a durable fabric, muted seascapes on the walls. Kelly folded her arms across her torso and hugged herself. Her boobs had been squished, prodded and subjected to an array of medical-imaging techniques, but she was trying not to think about it all—or watch the consultant's office door like a hawk.

At that moment a nurse emerged from the very same door and scanned the room of frowning women. Kelly held her breath.

'Samantha Dooley?' the nurse asked hopefully.

A girl in her twenties, two rows back, rose and followed the nurse inside.

Kelly exhaled again. This was torture. She turned to Chloe, who was sitting next to her studying a picture of a lighthouse on a balmy summer's day.

'Has Dan calmed down yet? I riled him up good and proper the other day.'

Chloe sighed. 'You really didn't have to talk to him on my behalf.'

Kelly recognised that weary tone. What Chloe really wanted to say was, *You should have minded your own business.*

'Sorry,' she mumbled. 'I think I was venting my frustration at the wrong man.'

Chloe shrugged and sighed again. 'Well, it did the trick—after a whole lot of shouting, we talked.'

'You did?'

'And then he showed me some pictures of Joshua.' She shook her head. 'I'd never even seen that photo album before, never even knew it existed....' She turned and looked at Kelly. 'I think it did him good to see them again, to share some of his memories.'

Kelly smiled at her sister-in-law. 'Do you think he's coming round?'

Chloe's head bobbed. 'He bristled a bit when I mentioned the support group I'd researched.'

Kelly snorted. 'I can imagine! My brother isn't one for group activities, especially touchy-feely type things. I imagine he'd rather flay himself alive than go to—' And then she realised she was trampling all over Chloe's careful plans and had to apologise again.

Chloe gave her a meaningful look. 'I know they're not Dan's "thing", but sometimes we can't do everything on our own. Sometimes we need to let people in so they can help us—you told Dan that yourself.'

Kelly breathed in. Yes, she had.

'He told me that you said he couldn't just stop living his life because he was scared of what the future might bring.'

Kelly nodded. 'Stuff happens, no matter what you do to try and protect yourself.' And wasn't she living proof of that? 'You just have to keep going, do what you need to survive.'

Chloe gave her a strange look. 'And what did *you* do to survive?'

Kelly frowned. She hadn't done anything. Just stayed strong and determined, had pushed her way through.

Dan's words came floating back to her. *That's the thing about greenhouses...*

But she wasn't anything like Dan! She hadn't shut her heart down and given up on love, as he had before he'd met Chloe. That option hadn't been open to her. She'd had her boys to keep her heart warm, and they'd needed a mother who could make up for their waste-of-space father.

As always, thinking of her ex made her angry. And she didn't want to be angry sitting here, staring at that smug-looking lighthouse.

A memory rose to the surface unbidden—the sleepless night she'd spent the week after Tim had moved out. How she'd made a silent vow to herself. How she'd told herself she'd never give anyone the opportunity to let her down that way again.

She realised she hadn't answered Chloe's question. 'I did what I needed to do at the time,' she said quietly, realising that had been true. Back then there had been no other way. But did that mean she needed to *keep* pushing everyone away?

Like she had Jason.

She hadn't really given him a chance, had she? She'd just shut down and done what she'd always done—prepared to survive. On her own.

She turned to her sister-in-law and her voice came out scratchy and wobbly. 'Oh, Chloe...I think I might have made the most horrible mistake!'

Before Chloe could even ask what she was talking about, the consultant's door opened again and the nurse walked a couple of steps into the waiting room.

'Kelly Bradford,' she said, with a rise of her eyebrows.

Jason had no idea where Kelly would be, just that she'd be at the hospital. That was all he'd managed to get from her tight-lipped brother. He didn't care. He'd flash a smile at anyone female with an ID card hanging round their neck and sweet-talk them into telling him where those tests were performed. Kelly should not have to be here on her own.

And, yes, he knew her sister-in-law was with her, but by 'on her own' he meant 'without him'.

But in the end he didn't need to smile at anyone, charm anyone. He stumbled across Kelly and the blonde he'd seen at the airport before he'd even walked inside a door. He spotted them, half-hidden by a small tree in a leafy little park labelled 'The Peace Garden' in the hospital grounds. The blonde was hugging Kelly tight and Kelly was sobbing uncontrollably.

The blonde looked startled when she spotted him striding towards her but, after the initial surprise had worn off, warmth crept into her eyes. She released Kelly and stepped away as Jason moved in and took her place. Kelly just kept sobbing, but the momentary hiccup the moment his arms slid around her told him she knew he was there. He pulled her close, almost crushing her, and whispered into her hair.

'It doesn't matter, Kelly. It doesn't matter what the doctors say. We'll fight it together.'

She nodded, even as her ribcage continued to heave, as the tears continued to fall. He was just still, held her until the gaps between oxygen-sucking breaths got longer. Then she wound both hands round his neck, pulled him to her and kissed him fiercely before pulling back and looking at him.

She was smiling at him through her tears. This woman was amazing. How had he even thought about letting her walk away from him? Such courage. Such strength. And he didn't care how much time they had left as long as they spent it together.

She said something in a hoarse, tear-ravaged voice that he didn't understand. His brain was having trouble making sense of the words.

'Jason, did you hear that…?'

He frowned and shook his head.

She took a deep breath, steadied herself and

looked him in the eye. 'It's just a cyst, that's all. Just a cyst.'

What did that mean? He couldn't have been looking any less confused because she grabbed him and kissed him again before saying, 'It's not cancer. I'm okay.'

And then they were back to kissing again and Jason didn't care one bit.

There was a soft cough behind him. 'I don't think you two need me anymore, so I'll just...be on my way.' Jason would have nodded and waved the sister-in-law goodbye if all his attention hadn't been tied up in showing Kelly just how wrong he'd been and just how *right* he was going to be in the future.

She came up for air eventually and rested her forehead against his. 'I'm sorry I shut you out.'

'I understand. But I want you to know you can count on me.'

She swallowed. 'You mean if...if something happens in the future?'

He nodded. 'I want to be with you, Kelly. Always. No matter what.'

She pulled back and he could see the joy at his words in her face. But he could also see the flicker of doubt in those cool grey-green eyes.

'I knew you'd need convincing,' he told her. 'So I did something. Something to show you I mean business.' He shook his head. 'I've spent too long skating on the top of life, pretending I was happy that way, pretending I wasn't missing anything by going deeper...'

She got his attention by hitting his chest softly with her open palm. 'Jason? What did you do...? You better not have done something to mess up that McGrath deal because I worked really hard on that and I will be most miffed!'

'Miffed?' He laughed. 'You don't have to be *miffed.*' Which was just as well because he was guessing that would involve a whole lot of ear-ache. 'I went to see my father, made the first step in patching things up.' He shook his head gently. 'It wasn't nearly as bad as I thought it would be...'

Her eyes widened. 'You did! Oh, Jason, that's brilliant.' Then she hit him again. Harder. 'And about time too!'

Well, he hadn't expected anything but truth that packed a punch from Kelly but, before she could do anything else violent, he pulled her close and kissed her again.

'I realised I'd checked out of my own life a long

time ago, but *you* made me want to check back in,'
he told her, keeping his arms firmly around her.
'Not for myself—although I know I need that—but
for you. I want to do it for you, because you woke
me up, Kelly. You gave me the kiss of life when
I was half-dead and didn't know I needed it. You
made me *want* to live again.'

'And you gave it right back to me,' she said,
grinning through her tears. 'Let's do it. If there's
one thing that this scare has taught me it's that
you have to grab every chance of happiness you
get. And you make me happy, Jason. I want to be
with you.'

He smiled back at her. 'It's a deal, then.' And
he pulled away, stepped back and offered her his
hand. She stared at it for a moment.

Kelly looked between his hand and his face a
few times, but she slid her fingers into his and his
larger ones closed around hers. He stopped smiling. This wasn't a joke or a cute gesture to make
her laugh. He was serious about this.

He knew she understood when her eyes filled
with tears. She nodded and the motion of her head
propelled them over the edge of her lashes and
down her cheeks. 'My problem isn't that I can't

commit,' he told her. 'I just chose not to for a very long time, but you know me well enough to know that when I make a deal I don't go back on it. Ever. You know what I'm saying, Kelly?'

Julie would be pleased. He was going to be able to tell her she needed to buy a new hat.

She nodded and smiled through her tears. 'It's a deal,' she whispered softly.

* * * * *